Strangling Man

'The victim's a nobody . . . it's what chummie did with the corpse that's causing the excitement. He left it draped over a gate . . .' Detective Chief Superintendent George Gently judged it a job for the locals, not for the big guns from Scotland Yard. Some affair involving fishermen, but with a single bizarre touch that might bring the press and the cameras running . . .

But he was wrong. Summoned to this village tragedy, one factor foremost among many baffled Gently: the phenomenal level of violence that had been employed. He had seen victims before who displayed the classical injuries of strangulation, but none like this. If the man had been garrotted, the bruising could not have been more savage. It seemed they were seeking a killer with a strength well-nigh superhuman, a man-gorilla.

At the centre of the extraordinary affair was Beattie Lound, 36, merry widow of pools-winning Aaron Lound, the honey-pot to which all the local bees made wing. So a line-up of local swains, all Beattie's actual or aspiring lovers, was paraded to Gently: Derek Jackson, much reviled garage owner; Markie Burrows, 20-year old love-lorn fisherman; Chick Shavers, ex-con and publican; Henry Gillings, strong near-silent cowman.

A chase by boat at dusk between the shoaly, tidal banks of the local waterways, a second corpse hanging over the gate (a further warning to every Don Juan in the place?) and the emergence of Esau Lound (six foot three, great shoulders, barrel-chest, ape-like arms. And of course the hands . . .). Had Gently found his strangling man?

With his usual apparently benign but steely probing of motives and his understanding of country people – their rivalries, passions, jealousies – Gently brings a formidable intelligence to the solving of a particularly complex, savage case.

Other murder cases investigated
by Chief Superintendent Gently, CID.

Gentle does it
Gently by the shore
Gently down the stream
Landed Gently
Gently through the mill
Gently in the sun
Gently with the painters
Gently to the summit
Gently go man
Gently where the roads go
Gently floating
Gently sahib
Gently with the ladies
Gently north-west
Gently continental
Gently coloured
Gently with the innocents
Gently at a gallop
Vivienne: Gently where she lay
Gently French
Gently in trees
Gently with love
Gently where the birds are
Gently instrumental
Gently to a sleep
The Honfleur decision
Gabrielle's way
Fields of heather
Gently between tides
Amorous Leander
The unhung man
'Once a prostitute . . .'
The Chelsea ghost
Goodnight, sweet prince

STRANGLING MAN

Alan Hunter

Constable London

First published in Great Britain 1987
by Constable & Company Limited
10 Orange Street, London WC2H 7EG

Set in 10/12 pt Linotron Palatino by
Rowland Phototypesetting Limited
Bury St Edmunds, Suffolk
Printed and bound in Great Britain by
St Edmundsbury Press Limited
Bury St Edmunds, Suffolk

British Library CIP data
Hunter, Alan, *1922–*
Strangling man.
I. Title
823'.914[F] PR6058.U52/

ISBN 0 09 468110 4

The character and events in this book are fictitious; the locale is sketched from life.

IN MEMORY

of Mrs Gertrude Emma Powell
of Lavengro, Oulton Broad,
Suffolk

1

A dark, damp, muggy, mid-October evening, fertile with the must of fallen leaves, and the few lights remaining across in the village dulled by mist.

Rising somewhere the twin-tower of the castle, the square tower of the church: sea-marks for seven centuries, but invisible tonight.

And no sound of the sea beyond the moorings, beyond the spit: the sea. No movement among forty, say, craft, streamed from their buoys by the ebb. And no lights, though a light there is here: the lighted window of a house. A house by itself, backed by tall trees, separated from the village by a field, trees; a house on a narrow road leading only to the marshes.

Alone.

And silently alone: except perhaps for the tap of falling leaves.

With a lighted window. While the lights of the village, one by one, are going out.

No wind, no sound of sea, no distant car.

No fall of foot.

So then a startling violence of light: the porch-light of the house switching on. And then, in a moment, the door opening, and a man letting himself out. A woman's voice, his low rejoinder, the door closing, clink of a chain; a man of solid build, his face harshly shadowed by the overhead light. He comes down a short drive to a creaking wicket-gate, pauses to look back at the house: sighs, when the porch-light vanishes, then turns to a car parked in the road.

But lights now – oh shattering lights!

Blue, red, white, orange lights.

Lights pulsing into the black sky, swivelling eyes in their sockets.

And a great clamp, an impossible clamp, a clamp that paralyses the lungs, a clamp that hands cannot tear away, crushing flesh, bone: crushing.

For seconds? Hours? Eternity?

And the firework sky becoming one great light.

And then no more.

A faint penumbra.

And nothing.

All switched off.

This leaves the downstair light in the house, which, shortly, is exchanged for one in a window above; and this, too, after a space, goes out, and there are no more lights in the narrow road. No lights, no sounds, except the tap of leaves in the spicy-smelling night. The scene is played, the world turns on, and the boats stream still on the ebb.

A peaceful night in a Suffolk village where, soon, all men of good will shall be asleep.

'Don't come in this morning, Gently – the County CID have a job for you.'

At Heatherings, on a Monday, breakfast was early, in anticipation of catching the train to town: they had barely sat down when the phone clamoured and the Assistant Commissioner (Crime) was on the line.

'The County CID . . . ?'

'Aspall is your man. Asks for you to meet him at the scene at Harford. Isn't that where they ran dope a few years back?'

'Well – yes.'

'As far as I have them, the details are these . . .'

At all events, the change in routine had met with the approval of Gabrielle, who was growing increasingly disinclined to quit Heatherings for their flat in town. Especially now, in a fine October, with the Walks quietly maturing in a sifted sun. Beside that, what was Holland Park and the rush and tumble of the capital?

'Is it a big case?'

'Doesn't sound that way.'

'Aha. But it may keep us here all the week?'

On the Friday their friends, the Capels, were giving a party for their son's birthday.

'Probably not. But we'll see.'

'At least you shall be back for lunch, yes? This place, Harford, it is not far?'

But he couldn't promise that, either.

To tell the truth, he was mildly surprised that the case had been handed to him at all: from what the AC (Crime) had been able to tell him, it was a job which the locals might well have handled. Some affair involving fishermen: it didn't call for big guns from Scotland Yard. Just a single bizarre touch that might bring the press and the cameras running . . .

Still, if that was what they wanted.

'I'll ring you from Harford.'

He had loitered over the papers before setting out. Aspall, the county CID boss, who he'd rung, hadn't been able to give him much more than the AC.

'The victim's a nobody . . . it's what chummie did with the corpse that's causing the excitement. He left it draped over a gate . . . the milkman found it there this morning.'

'Whose gate?'

'The girl-friend's. Barnby, that's his name, had spent the evening with her. I understand she's a bit of a merry widow, but I don't have other details. I'm off there now. May we expect you?'

Well: perhaps it did have some meat in it. But he didn't hurry, nonetheless, tooling the Rover along the twisty roads.

Harford was fourteen miles down the coast, once a small port, now decayed to a village; a lonely spot behind lonely roads, visited these days mostly by yachtsmen.

Though occasion had taken him there before he still needed to pull up to consult a map, so that it was getting towards mid-morning when he drifted past the first higgledy-piggledy cottages. A right turn took him into the small square that was the focus of the village: at one end the church, at the other trees over which peered the brick towers of a castle-keep. Then a few shops, houses, a couple of pubs – there really wasn't much to

Harford. And the small, flat-roofed police station in pink brick, its modest forecourt jammed with cars.

Also, people. They stood around in groups, keeping a little distance from the police station. And every eye was on the Rover as he double-parked, slammed the door, and went in.

'Has Superintendent Aspall arrived . . . ?'

A uniform man showed him into a cramped office. There Aspall and two other men were poring over photographs spread on a desk. Aspall introduced the men: County's case-i/c, a Detective-Inspector Slatter, and the station sergeant, Bartram, a heavy-featured man with anxious eyes.

'The trouble is, word's got round . . .'

'They think there's a nutter loose, sir,' Slatter said. 'That milkman who found him spread it about, and now the whole village is stirred up.'

Aspall said: 'It wasn't a pretty sight. The man looked as though he'd been strangled by a maniac. And he was no lightweight – see here, sir. You'd say he was a man who could handle himself.'

He pushed the photographs across the desk. Three showed the body slung over a painted field-style gate. Slung precisely, at the point of balance, hands reaching down one side to feet at the other. Then two of the distorted face, the bulging eyes, the straining mouth; and the neck one huge black bruise. A man of forty, thereabouts, perhaps six feet. With big gnarled hands.

'Barnby could handle himself, sir,' Bartram said. 'A couple of drinks and he was trouble. I could believe in a nutter myself when I saw him hanging over that gate.'

'What did the doctor say?'

'Been dead several hours, sir, maybe around midnight, he wouldn't be certain. But one thing he did say. The chummie who did it must have hands like grappling hooks.'

'No witnesses.'

'None we've turned up.'

'The lady he'd been with?'

'Mrs Lound, sir. She didn't hear a thing. Says she saw him out at half-past eleven, did a job in the kitchen, then went up to bed.'

'She lives alone?'

'Yes sir. And now she's plaguing us for protection.'

Gently brooded over the photographs. Violence . . . and violence of a manic degree. Violence of an order not commonly met with: if the neck had been broken, no surprise. He shuffled the photographs together.

'So now the rest of the picture! I want to know everything about this pair – Barnby, the lady, friends, associates and all you've turned up to date. Any obvious suspects?'

Bartram looked still more anxious.

'As I was telling the Super and the Inspector, sir! I don't want to blacken any characters, but with Mrs Lound . . . well, there it is.'

'You mean she had other men?'

'Just a few, sir.'

Aspall said: 'More than a few, from what I've been hearing. Anything in trousers was fair game. Like we may have to check out the whole neighbourhood. She has money too, hasn't she?'

'Money too, sir.'

'So there's your angle,' Aspall said. 'Let's say Barnby was leading the field, and one of his rivals put the boot in.'

'Well I don't know, sir,' Bartram said. 'That was a funny old way to put the boot in.'

'Someone did it, was capable of it.'

Bartram stared at the photographs, said nothing.

Gently said: 'Let's order up coffee. Then I want a full rundown.'

Coffee was fetched by a pink-faced constable who was clearly impressed by the brass in the office – probably, not since the station was commissioned had rank of this altitude paid it a visit.

A cramped little room in a doll's house of a place, run by Bartram and three uniform men. Outside, the reception area could scarcely cope with the legs that County had drafted in.

A tiny police station in a lonely village by a tidal river: and the presence of the sea.

'Now then. The lady first.'

He had taken Bartram's chair at the desk as of right. Aspall and the lean, taut-faced Slatter had bagged the other two, leaving Bartram to stand like a naughty schoolboy.

Gently's pipe was going. Through the window he could see the square without, the knots of staring villagers.

'Well, she was Aaron Lound's missus, sir.'

'Who was Aaron Lound.'

'He was one of the fishermen. They work the river here, one or two of them, netting the drains right up to Thwaite. That's the creeks, sir, in the flats and the marshes – they work the tides, and get some fair old catches.'

'So who was she?'

'Maiden name of Willey. The Willeys kept The Mariners, near the quay. She was brought up to serve in the bar, which no doubt is where Lound met her. So then they married and set up house in one of the cottages down there.'

'There was mention of money.'

'A win on the pools, sir.'

'Much?'

'Yes sir. Lound hit the jackpot.'

'A big win.'

'That's what they say, sir. And there was no more fishing after that. Lound sold his boat, bought a posh car, and moved to that house where she's living now. It stands across the playing-field, on a back road, and you can see the sea from some of the windows.'

Which you couldn't do from the village, where the spit hid the sea from view.

'So what happened to him, this husband?'

'Coming to him, sir.' Bartram was sweating. 'It wasn't anything you could call comic, just what you might expect from a man like Lound. He sold his boat, but he bought a yacht, a thirty-six-foot Hillyard sloop. And then he started to get these ideas about making a trip around the world.'

'Around the world!'

'Yes sir.'

Gently puffed. 'And that's what he did?'

'Yes sir. Come Easter, it'll be seven years ago. I was down there to see him off – he had a band playing, all sorts of malarkey.'

'How far did he get?'

'His last cable was from Panama. From there he set out to cross the Pacific, but he never made it to the islands. They reckoned the typhoon season was due and that his sloop never stood a chance. A tanker sighted some wreckage south of the Galapagos, and that was the end of Aaron Lound.'

'Leaving his widow sitting pretty,' Aspall said.

'Very pretty, sir,' Bartram said.

'Is she a looker too?'

'Some would call her a dish, sir. And then only thirty when it happened.'

Aspall whistled. 'They must have been queuing up. The marvel is there hasn't been trouble before. And she's been a widow for six years?'

'And six months,' Bartram said. 'Only marrying again wasn't what she had in mind.'

'She strung them along.'

'Well, there you are, sir. She likes the men, no doubt about it. And she had the looks, had the money, so I suppose you can hardly blame her. She had to keep her nose clean while Aaron was alive, but once he'd gone she cut loose – a lot of parties and wild goings-on, though she's sobered up a bit since. Just lately it's been quieter up there – for Beattie Lound, that is.'

'Meaning,' Aspall said.

Bartram twitched his shoulders.

'More like one at a time, these days.'

'Barnby?'

'That's what she's telling us. But if you listen to the gossip you may hear different.'

Gently said: 'So let's hear about Barnby.'

'Yes sir.'

Bartram shuffled his feet, stood a little straighter. Clearly he was unused to being the centre of so much high-powered attention.

'Like I said, sir, he could be a handful when he had a few inside him, though no worse than some I could name. I don't know of him having any enemies.'

'He was one of the fishermen.'

'Right, sir. Had his own boat these several years. Got enough put away to buy a house in Harbour Road when he got married a few years back.'

'Then there's a Mrs Barnby?'

'Separated, sir, and no need to guess why. She took off back to her people, who keep the post-office stores at Nettlesham. That was in the summer. I can't say how long before that he was carrying on. She took the two little kids with her and they say she's put in for a divorce.'

'So then his affair with Mrs Lound was serious.'

'He may have thought it was, sir. But Mrs Lound won't have it, says the idea of him marrying her was a joke.'

'She had made that clear to him?'

'Says so, sir.'

'But still he was making regular visits?'

Bartram hesitated. 'You mean, like he might have been standing in someone else's light?'

'Just like that.'

Aspall said: 'The more I hear about this, the more certain I am. Six years there's been violence brewing over that woman, and last night it came to a head. That's the picture. Because why else would chummie have left the body hanging over her gate?'

'A sort of warning, sir,' Slatter put in.

'You're damned right it was a warning – to every other Don Juan in the place. And that probably explains the brutality of it. Chummie wanted the message to stick.'

'A big 'un,' Slatter said. 'He has to be big.'

'Big, violent and round the twist.'

'There can't be many around like him, sir, in a place like this. He has to stand out.'

And just then came a tap on the door, and a ginger-haired DC pushed his head round.

'Sir. We've got an informant out here.'

'An informant?'

'Yes sir. Fellow called Spratt. Says he can finger chummie for us. Says it's the bloke who owns the garage.'

'Who owns the garage . . .'

Bartram was staring with unbelieving eyes.

Aspall said: 'Does it add up – is he a big fellow, a likely customer?'

'Yes, but –'

'A pal of Mrs Lound's?'

'Well, she'll be a customer – I am myself.'

'So,' Aspall said.

Coming out of his stupor, Bartram rapped to the DC:

'Fetch that miserable so-and-so in here!'

Spratt was nudged in: a thin, pasty-faced youth in a ragged leather jacket and oily jeans. He shrank away from the towering Bartram, whose heavy face was red with anger.

'So – you again, Spratt!'

'Look, I'm only trying to help –'

'Sonny, not another word from you until you've told these gentlemen your credentials!'

'But what's that got to do –'

'Just tell them.'

Spratt said sulkily: 'So I worked for Derek, didn't I?'

'And,' Bartram snapped, 'And –'

'Got the sack,' Spratt mumbled.

'Got the sack,' Bartram said. 'For nicking gear from the garage stores. Should have been done, and only wasn't because Jackson wouldn't press charges. Those are the credentials of sonny there. Now perhaps we can hear what he has to say.'

'I know what I know,' Spratt said. 'That's all.'

'It had better be good, sonny,' Bartram said.

'So they had a fight, didn't they,' Spratt said. 'Behind the garage. Him and Luke. Luke give him a black eye.'

'Luke being Barnby,' Bartram said. 'And what were they fighting about, sonny?'

'About her, wasn't it?'

'About Mrs Lound?'

'Course. They were both having it away.'

'Both?'

'What I said. All the time I worked there. Fancied Derek, she did. Fancied a lot of blokes, didn't she?'

'I can think of one she wouldn't,' Bartram said. 'When did this mill take place sonny?'

'Last week. Before I was sacked. Why he wouldn't do me, like I knew too much. Luke came round there late, when we were finishing a job, said if Derek didn't lay off her he'd finish up in hospital. And Derek swore at him, said he'd have her, that Luke was the one they'd cart away. Then they set about each other round the back. And Luke give him a black eye.'

'No witnesses,' Bartram said. 'Just you, sonny.'

'Got a black eye,' Spratt said. 'You could see it.'

'No customers for petrol just then.'

'I tell you, it was late,' Spratt said.

'And all the time you worked there he was chasing Mrs Lound?'

'Afternoons,' Spratt said. 'Sometimes evenings. Ask Markie Burrows. Markie's seen him coming out there.'

'Markie Burrows,' Bartram said. 'Markie told you. And that's all you know about it, sonny-boy.'

'No, I seen him go off there, haven't I?'

'He told you where?' Bartram said.

Spratt licked his lips.

Bartram glanced at Gently. 'What do you reckon, sir?'

Gently shrugged, pulled on his pipe. Spratt was probably the first tale-bearer of many – and anonymous phone calls, they'd be coming in soon. Yet somewhere one had to start on the haystack.

'We'll hold him for further questioning.'

Bartram summoned the DC, and Spratt was removed.

Gently said: 'You say Jackson is a big fellow?'

'Never been in any trouble, sir,' Bartram said.

Aspall said: 'Shall we look him over, sir?'

Outside, Gently saw a face he thought he knew.

Three pumps, a small office and a gaping barn made up the total of Jackson's Garage, with a small bungalow behind, surrounded by fields still scarred from stubble-burning. Four cars stood waiting attention on the oil-stained gravel fore-court, five others, with prices affixed to their screens, stood lined up before the barn.

The place lay remote, on the outskirts of the village, with the first cottages hidden by a turn in the road.

'Mr Jackson?'

'Just a minute . . . I'll see!'

A woman wearing an apron had emerged from the office.

Now she hastened into the barn where, in the gloom, a car stood over a pit from which emerged sparks.

Aspall murmured: 'It could stand a rich widow, here.'

The cars lined up for sale appeared to be bangers. Then, behind, the modest bungalow showed flaking paint, while its garden was a tangled wilderness. The woman returned.

'He'll be here.'

An oily figure was climbing out of the pit. A large man, clad in grease-stiff overalls. He cut the arc of a welder before advancing towards them.

'Yes . . . ?'

'Derek Jackson?'

He just stared, with narrowed eyes. Grease-smudged features, tousled hair: large, blackened hands.

'Police.'

'Who bloody else?'

'You were expecting us?'

'Maybe. Who are you?'

Gently told him. All the while he was wiping the black hands on his overall.

'Spratt, was it?'

'Spratt . . . ?'

'Spratt who sent you after me! I know that young devil. He'd drop me in it if he could. So what do you want?'

'We are investigating the death of Luke Barnby.'

'Then why come to me.'

'If we could go inside?'

He hesitated, glancing at the office, through the window of which the woman was staring avidly. Then he nodded to the bungalow, led the way to a yawing gate.

The door was unlocked; they went through a hall to a sitting-room, shabbily furnished. Jackson went to the window for a moment to stare back at the office. He turned to them.

'Look! I can guess what that louse told you, but I don't have anything to hide. I was out there working all the evening.'

Gently said: 'And after that?'

'Had a bite and went to bed, didn't I.'

'Do you live here alone?'

'So what? No sod can prove I was anywhere else.'

'They can't prove you were here, either.'

Jackson glared at him through his grime. Beneath it was a good-looking face with a broad, stubbly jaw. Also, a faintly discoloured eye.

Gently said: 'A week ago. Barnby came out here to see you. Threats passed between you. There was a fight. Do you deny any of this?'

'That bloody little tick.'

'But do you deny it?'

He looked as though he would like to.

'All right, we were slinging words at each other, but that doesn't mean we really meant them.'

'Who won the fight?'

'Never you mind. It had nothing to do with last night.'

'You have heard where Barnby was found?'

'I said never mind! Last night I was here, and that's not there.'

'Though you often were there.'

The black hands clenched.

'I could do for someone right now! And to think I only gave the little squirt a job because his mother begged me to take him on. So if I was, then?'

'It was you and Barnby. Making the running. Turn about. Coming to threats, and then to blows. Coming finally to last night.'

'But I wasn't there.'

'Which you can't prove.'

'Look, at ten o'clock I made a phone call.'

'It doesn't cover you.'

'Oh, bloody hell.'

He thumped his fists against the wall. Over at the office, a glint of spectacles betrayed the woman's face, peering round the corner.

'Listen, I'm admitting all the rest. I've been going with Beattie for a year. All right, I know she has others, that's her way, but we were special. Only bloody Barnby wouldn't have it, wanted Beattie on his own. He beat up another bloke, no more than a kid, because he was always hanging round there. And me he was after more than the rest, because he knew I was Beattie's steady. Yes, we had a bloody fight. Likely would have had some more.'

His breath came quick, he glared at Gently, at the aloof Aspall, the sharp-eyed Slatter.

Gently said: 'You were in his way.'

'Too bloody right I was.'

'And he was in yours.'

'So what?'

'Now he isn't in anyone's way.'

'So that's how it goes. But I didn't do it. I was here on my tod, you prove different.'

'And if you were seen down in the village?'

He stared, mouth gaping for a moment.

'Who says that?'

Gently shrugged.

'It's that bastard Spratt again, isn't it?'

'Is it?'

'Just let me catch him – maybe he'll be hanging over someone's gate!'

'Like Luke Barnby.'

'Yes – like Barnby. That's what you want me to say, isn't it?'

Now the black hands hung open, crooked, and the narrowed eyes scowled at Gently.

'You're a rotten so-and-so, aren't you? You're going to put someone away for this. Doesn't matter who, as long as the face fits and the poor sod hasn't a leg to stand on. Well, it won't be me. All you've got against me is what a lying little toad has told you.'

Gently said: 'And what have you got, Jackson?'

'Bastard,' Jackson said. 'Bastard.'

Aspall said: 'Any more of that, Jackson, and you'll be inside for insulting behaviour. Last night, you weren't here all the time, were you?'

'Find out,' Jackson snarled.

'When we do,' Aspall said. 'Your feet won't touch.'

Jackson glared at him, his hands working.

'You meant to have her,' Aspall said. 'Her and her money.'

Jackson turned his head. Spat.

Then the woman came running, gesturing to the window.

'You're wanted on the phone . . . !'

Jackson went.

Aspall said: 'I have an instinct about this one. Shall we take him with us, sir?'

Gently stared after the departing man, shook his head.

'Not yet.'

'Sir, he's big enough, bad enough,' Slatter urged.

'He won't run. And we need more leverage. Perhaps we can get it from the widow.'

Slatter didn't look hopeful.

'I'll put men on it, sir. And maybe have a word with the woman on the pumps.'

They left the bungalow. They could see Jackson at the telephone. In his haste, he had knocked the yawing gate off its hinge.

2

'Where was the body taken?'

'To our morgue at HQ, sir.'

'Get me the morgue on the phone.'

Aspall had left, Gently was checking through the few reports that had come in. The area around the Lound house had been searched as a priority, yielding little but two cigarette-ends; though these, found in a gateway to the playing-field opposite, suggested that a watcher might have stationed himself there. Slatter himself had been to Barnby's residence, but had found nothing that threw any light on the tragedy. Witnesses there were none. The pubs had turned out well before Barnby had met his killer.

'Chief Superintendent Gently. The body from Harford. I want a special check on the area of bruising. Any alien substance you can find there, but especially grease, and grease mixed with carbon . . . yes, ring me at Harford, whether you get a result or not.'

Meanwhile, Slatter had summoned his men and dispatched them to enquire after sightings of Jackson.

'Just a bit of luck, sir, and we'll have him to rights . . .'

In the square, the groups of gapers were thinning out. But already it was probably on the grape-vine that Jackson was the man the police had their eyes on. A smear of grease, a single sighting! Then, to quote Aspall, his feet wouldn't touch. But if neither? If the black night had hidden him, and the hands that crushed Barnby's throat were gloved . . . ? Gently sighed to himself.

'Let's talk to the widow.'

At Heatherings, Gabrielle would be brewing coffee. Here, the low sun, now clear of mist, shone like an eye on the naked village.

The junction of the back road to the marshes lay conveniently close to Jackson's Garage: clearly its proprietor could have gone that way with few or no eyes upon him. Within a hundred yards one came to the playing-field, with a view across it of the village houses; then, on the right, a wooded knoll, and nestling below it a house.

'That's her place.'

Gently halted the Rover. The house stood in a garden with high, unkempt hedges. A typical product of the thirties, red brick below, rough-cast above, pantiles, a broad chimney-breast, porch, twin bay windows. Beside it a brick-built garage with a gate between it and the house. Then a dozen yards of weedy gravel to a white-painted field-gate, with an iron wicket-gate beside it. Fairwinds, said a painted name-board. Against the garage was propped a lady's bicycle.

'He was facing the house, sir . . . his feet this side.'

The gate was fascinating Slatter. In the playing-field, at a little distance, a few worthies had been watching the Rover pull in. The field was fringed with poplars, yellow in the sun, had a gateway nestling in evergreen shrubs: rough, untended, with one derelict goal-post, the backs of the houses two hundred yards off. And the road? That dipped away to a prospect of marshes and glinting water. And the trees behind the house were oaks and chestnuts, the latter fiery with autumn tints.

'At what time was he found?'

The cover offered by the evergreens was perhaps thirty yards from the gate of the house. Even closer, and on the same side, was a niche in the overgrown hawthorn hedge.

'About seven, sir. We got straight out here. Bartram had closed off the road and the field.'

'Was the garden searched?'

'Yes sir. And all the ground up to those trees.'

At a venture, Gently drove on, came soon to the road's end at a gate. There red-and-white bullocks paused to gaze at them, the russet marsh stretched away to tidal waters. He turned and drove back. A woman wearing a headscarf was pushing the bicycle through the wicket-gate. As they parked, she mounted and rode away. Another woman was standing in the porch.

'So they've called in the brass, have they? Well, well! Who said Harford wasn't on the map?'

But the tone of her voice was not facetious, nor the stare of her fierce brown eyes. Around five-feet six, strong-built, broad features framed with chestnut hair: a snubbed nose. And the voice deep and plangent, her weight behind it.

Dressed – swathed – in a flower-patterned gown with a low neck and split skirt.

'From just up the road, aren't you – is that why they've put you on it? The one with the French missus. I've heard Chick tell the tale about you.'

'Chick . . . ?'

'Chick and Myrtle Shavers, who used to be at The Eel's Foot. Well, they've got Dad's old pub now. A real friend of yours he says he is.'

The face among the gapers.

'Shall we go in, Mrs Lound?'

She swept him with a glance.

'You can call me Beattie.'

She showed them through a hall to a lounge furnished with voluminous chairs and a vast settee. For a day quite mild the room was overheated and had also a sickly smell of fresh polish. On the walls, cheap framed reproductions. In the unused grate, bulrushes. Then, in a corner, a bar with a fair collection of bottles.

'I suppose I daren't offer you gents a drink?'

She poured herself one however: a straight gin. She took a nip before demanding:

'Well – have you got the bloke yet?'

'Shall we sit down?'

'But I want to know. I mean, it's all very well for you lot, but I'm a woman living here on my own. So what are you going to do?'

Gently said: 'I doubt if you are at risk, Mrs Lound.'

'Not at risk! With Dracula outside there, still running around loose?'

'I believe he intends no harm to you.'

'No, he only left Lukey hanging over my gate.'

'That was meant as a warning.'

'A warning . . . to me?'

'Perhaps to you. But more likely to others.'

The brown eyes were clinging to his.

'The bastard,' she said. 'Who is it?'

Gently said: 'A man who I think is well known to you.'

'But Christ . . . who is he?'

'Shall we sit down?'

They sat. Mrs Lound chose the settee; mechanically, the legs were tucked up, displayed. Slatter fell backwards into one of the huge chairs: Gently seated himself with more decorum. He said:

'May we be quite frank about your men friends?'

For an instant, the eyes were fierce.

'Barnby wasn't the only one, was he?'

'Are you asking me or telling me?'

'I would like you to tell me.'

'I'll bet you would.' She gave a nervous laugh. 'So who are you on about now?'

'Is there more than one?'

'Suppose there is. That's for me to know and you to find out.'

'You want us to catch this man, don't you?'

She played with the glass. 'Just what are you getting at?'

Gently said: 'Barnby had a rival. A man he clearly believed to pose a threat.'

Now the eyes had gone still. 'Who is it?'

'I think you know very well, Mrs Lound.'

'You want me to grass on someone, is that it?'

'I want you to tell me about Derek Jackson.'

'Derek!'

Was there relief in the eyes? She tossed back the drink.

'You can't be serious. Not Derek! Lukey didn't bother Derek. And I was about through with Lukey, anyway.'

'So why wouldn't you name Jackson to me?'

'Because it's too stupid, that's why.'

'Because you are seeking to protect him?'

'Oh, lay off. Why should I send you after Derek?'

She scrambled up, went back to the bar, poured herself a fresh drink: poured with a barmaid's flourish. Then returned to her seat.

'You want to hear about Derek?'

Gently watched her, saying nothing.

'I bought my new car from him – August of last year, when the date letter changed. I knew he fancied me, of course, but he was shy, would you believe it? A hunk like him. He took me on a test run and wasn't going to lay a hand on me. Well, we changed all that, didn't we. I found a nice quiet spot for us to park in. And he's a real devil when you get to know him. But strangle Lukey? That's a laugh.'

Gently said: 'Have you been in his company lately?'

'What has that got to do with it?'

'He had a black eye. Did you notice?'

'So if I did. That was last week.'

'How did he explain it?'

She drank. 'Told me a wrench slipped and caught him. Now are you going to tell me something different?'

'He got the black eye in a fight with Barnby.'

She stared. 'A fight?'

'Over you, Mrs Lound. Barnby wanted Jackson to give you up.'

She gave a gurgling chuckle. 'I don't believe it! A fight over me? You're having me on.'

'We have Jackson's statement.'

'They fought over me?'

'Also the testimony of an eye-witness.'

'Well, well.'

She hung her head, gurgled again.

'He was going for broke, I know, Lukey, that was why I was handing him his cards. But I didn't think I'd given him enough encouragement for him to go beating up other blokes. He was after the dough, Lukey. Though he wasn't so bad either.'

Gently said: 'And Jackson?'

'What about him?'

'Wouldn't he have expectations too?'

'Don't be daft. He's just a hunk. He knows it won't be going any further.' She drank. 'I've had marriage, you know. That's him on the wall, Aaron. A right bastard. He'd have knocked me about if he'd caught me giving the eye. But what is life? If you've got it you may as well use it, that's what I say.'

'And that has been your philosophy for six years?'

'You don't get my sort of luck every day.'

'And no trouble before this?'

She gurgled. 'With wives, mostly. I never have any trouble with men.'

She fetched the photograph from the wall and stood by while Gently examined it. The print showed a large-featured, hook-nosed man with accusing eyes and a stern mouth. Victorian almost: it was probably true that marriage to him had produced small joy. She hung it back on the wall.

'So now you know.'

'Barnby. Jackson. There must be others besides them.'

Her eyes mocked him. 'What do you think? I don't cut notches on the door. I'd got a few years to make up, hadn't I. But don't go getting wrong ideas. If I knew the bloke you were looking for, I'd come out with it, don't you worry.'

'Then who else has been here – lately?'

'No one. Well . . . not regular.'

'But others?'

'You know how it is. Now and then you take a fancy.'

'Names would help.'

'It's too stupid. Once in a blue moon I bring someone back. But I can't see any of them hanging around to strangle Lukey.' She paused. 'All right, then. Your pal Shavers.'

'Shavers!'

She leered. 'Not a word to Myrtle! Then there's Markie, young Markie Burrows. Though I was more like a mother to him.'

Slatter said: 'Spratt mentioned a Burrows, sir.'

'Once,' Mrs Lound said. 'Just the once. Baby-snatching isn't my line. Only sometimes you're feeling maternal.'

'Burrows is a youngster?'

'Maybe he's twenty. He lives with his mother in one of the cottages. Works an old boat covered with patches and scratches a living with it somehow.' She giggled. 'He'd loaf around out there, never daring to catch my eye. Then one day Lukey left early to catch a tide, and I opened the door and beckoned to him. Oh dear! I'll bet he didn't tell his old battle-axe of a mother.'

Gently said: 'Where might we find him?'

'Go on. You can't imagine Markie doing a thing like this.'

'But if I wanted him?'

'At the yard, like as not. Putting another patch on his boat.'

'Does he smoke?'

'I've seen him with a fag.'

'Would you have seen him last night?'

She shook her head.

And Burrows was the only recent 'fancy' she'd admit to, Shavers, the one before, dating three weeks back. About the rest she was cagey: they were past history; just lately it had stopped at the deceased and Jackson.

'But what about giving me some protection?'

Slatter assured her that a police presence would continue.

'You couldn't spare me a bloke – like to sleep here?'

They left her in the porch, watching their departure.

Slatter said slyly: 'She had her eye on you, sir!'

Gently grunted and tooled the Rover away. In the playing-field, the gapers had begun moving off, except for one old man, who sat eating sandwiches.

Downstream for a quarter of a mile the yachts lay swung, bows to flood; then there was the quay with some lifting-machinery; and upstream a raffle of beached boats, huts, nets, and tangles of gear.

Gently parked by a notice that forbade parking and, together with Slatter, strolled up the bank. Mrs Lound had spoken true: a tall youth in smock and jeans was just then slapping bitumastic on a much-repaired boat. He glanced towards the two approaching men, but went on with what he was doing.

'Mark Burrows?'

'That's me, then.'

Tall, slim: but heavy of bone. He had fair-complexioned, almost girlish features, with a Cupid-bow mouth and straight pale hair. His eyes also were of pallid hue, giving him overall a drained, colourless appearance.

'Police. Just a few questions. Where do you say you were last night?'

'Last night? But I told the other man –'

'So now I'd like you to tell me. Shall we say, from 7.00 p.m. onwards?'

The pale eyes didn't want to meet Gently's.

'I was in The Mariners, you ask them, right through till closing time.'

'And then?'

'Well . . . I went home, didn't I. Didn't want my mother waiting up. She'll tell you, I was home before eleven, she'd have made a fuss if I'd been later.'

'You were home by eleven?'

'Yes, I was home.'

'Where do you live?'

'Just up the road. Church Cottages, number six. That's only a few yards from the pub.'

'You walked home alone?'

'Yes . . . I suppose so. The other blokes . . . yes, I was alone.'

'Though the pub was just turning out?'

'Well, they hung about. I drank up, went straight home.'

'Have you your cigarettes on you?'

'I . . . yes.'

The sudden switch had him staring.

'May I see them?'

He struggled awkwardly with the smock; came up with a crushed pack of Benson & Hedges. Gently glanced at Slatter. Slatter nodded. Gently said:

'I don't want to make this hard for you. But I think that at some time last night you were in the vicinity of Mrs Lound's house.'

'No, I wasn't.'

'Not last night?'

'No. I was never there at all.'

'But you have been there.'

'No!'

'We have it on the testimony of Mrs Lound. She says you have a habit of hanging about there, and that once she invited you in.'

'Oh dear!'

Just for a moment, Gently thought the young man might cut

and run. He had flushed to the ears, and was trying to throw down the brush which, however, had stuck to his fingers. His eyes were rolling.

'It – it wasn't anything. She shouldn't have said that.'

'But you were invited in?'

'Yes – no, it was something she wanted fixed . . .'

No question about it.

'And you are often up there?'

'No. Not often . . . what did she say?'

'And again last night?'

'She just wanted . . .'

'Someone who smokes these cigarettes was there.'

He stared helplessly at the battered packet, and then appealingly at Gently. He couldn't have been much over eighteen: he had a look of a child who had been caught out.

Gently said: 'We've talked to your mate, Spratt, and to Derek Jackson from the garage. What Spratt says confirms Mrs Lound's testimony that you spend a good deal of time up there. And what Jackson says suggests you may have had trouble with Luke Barnby.'

'I play football up there –'

'After dark?'

'I never had any trouble with Luke.'

'He didn't catch you up there, give you a pasting, tell you to stop pestering Mrs Lound?'

'He was like that – it wasn't only me!'

'But he did catch you up there.'

'No . . . on the playing-field.'

'In the gateway of the playing-field. Nearly opposite the house. Where you hoped she might see you and ask you in again.'

'No!'

'And where you were last night, watching, while Barnby was in the house.'

His colour was coming and going, and still he was struggling with the brush. Slatter was observing him with interest, a connoisseur of these occasions. Young and green: and with the image of a battle-axe mother at his elbow . . .

Gently said: 'You were there. All we want to know is what you saw.'

'No. I wasn't there. I was in the pub, like I said.'
'Who else did you see there?'
'I didn't see anyone –'
'A man you knew.'
'No.'
'Then he was a stranger.'
'I tell you nobody. Nobody at all!'
'You waited in the gateway, smoked two cigarettes. Barnby's car was parked outside. It was dark and quiet, you could hear sounds, perhaps sometimes hear them in the house. What did you hear?'
'I keep telling you! I was in the pub all the evening.'
'We shall check on that.'
'I wasn't there, don't know anything about it.'
'And you were home by eleven?'
'Yes I was. Ask – ask my mother. I was home.'
'We shall ask her.'
It almost broke him. At last he succeeded in getting rid of the brush, threw it down under the boat, grabbed for an old jacket that hung over the gunnel.
'Look, I've got to get home to my lunch . . .'
'Wait.'
'I've told you all I know!'
Then he ducked his head and bolted, the jacket flapping behind him.
'The young devil!' Slatter exclaimed. 'Do you want me to fetch him back, sir?'
Gently shrugged, shook his head.
'Perhaps you'll have a word with his mother. Oh, and saliva tests on those fag-ends.'
Slatter stared. 'You don't fancy him, sir . . . ?'
'So far, he's the only one we can link to the spot.'
'But . . . all the same, sir.'
Yes, all the same: could one imagine that young man crushing Barnby's throat?

Slatter went about his errands, Gently collected his car from the quay; ambled it past the old warehouse, now a chandlery, and into the yard of The Mariners public house. Almost at once a door opened at the back and a man came, half-running, across to the car.

'Give me a minute, Chiefy, for chrissake, before you show your face in there . . . !'

'Get in, Shavers.'

'Listen, I don't know a blind thing about it. But one bleeding hint to Myrtle, and well, you know where that will land me . . . !'

Chick Shavers, ex-con, now the husband of the landlady: who'd had to perform some quick footwork on a previous occasion. Slim, with slicked hair, in sweater, slacks and suede shoes. Sharp, close-set eyes: now fixed anguishedly on Gently.

'Honest, I was in the bar all night – ask any of the geezers in there – and then I was upstairs with Myrtle, just as soon as I'd got in the glasses.'

'Myrtle is your wife, Chick.'

'Oh come on, Chiefy! You know she wouldn't tell fibs for me. Only don't bloody ask her, that's all – just do me a favour, please.'

'I've been talking to Beattie.'

As though worked by a spring, Shavers' head jerked round to glance towards the pub.

'Just don't mention that bint's name! Myrtle won't believe now that I wasn't after her.'

'Because you were, Chick.'

'All right, all right – me and a couple of dozen others. But not for weeks. I had to lay off when Myrtle found some hairs on my jacket. The silly cow dyes her hair red, and I had to spin this yarn about a ginger tom-cat.'

'Did Myrtle swallow it?'

'You know women. I hardly dare pull a pint for a bird these days. But it's over, I'm telling you, washed up, and I haven't been back there for a month.'

'Three weeks.'

'So three weeks. You're never after me for this one, Chiefy?'

'You were one of her boy-friends.'

'Oh, for crying out. Show me someone round here who wasn't.'

Gently smiled at the distant castle.

'Just now what I'm after is a pint and some sandwiches. Oh,

and a measure of co-operation. And I'm expecting to get both.'

Shavers stared hard at him. 'And no word to Myrtle?'

'Tell her we're talking over old times.'

'Yeah,' Shavers said. 'Yeah. I've said it before, Chiefy, and I'll say it again. You and me speak the same language.'

The refreshment arrived; Gently pushed his seat back and took a long pull from his glass. Over at a window, two hard, intent eyes seemed to be trying to bore into the car. And Shavers was squeezing down low in his seat, his back turned towards the window.

'So what do you want to know, Chiefy?'

'You have a customer called Mark Burrows.'

'That nana. A bleeding mother's boy. Couldn't see him doing a case like Barnby.'

'Says he was here last night till closing.'

'Then he's a lying git, isn't he? He was here all right, along with some mates. But not when we slung them out he wasn't.'

'Can you say when he left?'

'Do me a favour. Sunday night it's all go. In the season we get them off the boats, too, and then you can hardly move in there.'

'He was drinking.'

'A couple of halves. That's the size of Markie Burrows.'

'Who was he with?'

'I'll ask round, Chiefy. Couldn't give you names off the cuff.'

Gently chewed; drank. 'Three weeks ago. When you were still on with Beattie Lound.'

'Don't mention that sodding name, Chiefy!'

'Did you see Burrows hanging round there then?'

Shavers' stare was sharp. 'She was never on with him?'

'Did you see him?'

'Once or twice. But stone me, he'd have run a mile if Beattie had given him the old green.'

'Barnby. Jackson.'

'I steered clear of them.' He lowered his voice. 'It was afternoons with me, wasn't it? You know the game, I was down at the yacht. Got me out of a few, that has.'

'Any others you can name?'

Shavers shook his head. 'But Burrows – you're having me on, aren't you?'

Gently ate, drank.

'And you're out to bust him?'

Gently ate, drank some more. He said: 'Last night. You had the usual crowd here?'

'Usual Sunday-nighters, Chiefy. One bloke from the boats, a big bearded punter. Only the season's over now.'

'Any other strangers?'

'One I didn't know. A rough-looking cove who niffed of cow-dung. He had a quick pint and scapa'd. I saw the punter's yacht go off this morning.'

'And Burrows wasn't there when you turned out.'

'Would I tell you a lie, Chiefy? I served his second half, it was eight or after, and never laid eyes on him after that. Closing time there were only a few in there, and Markie Burrows wasn't one of them.'

Gently drank up. 'Keep me posted, Chick. Remembering that we speak the same language.'

'And you won't split to Myrtle?'

Gently handed him his glass and plate. Then spun his engine.

In the street, he was waved down by Slatter, who had a young DC in tow.

'Sir, a bit of a turn-up! Barnby's missus has let on that her brother was looking for Barnby last night. Barnby had been pestering her to see the kids, and her brother came here to sort him out.'

'Do we have the brother?'

'I'm having him fetched, sir. He works on a farm just up the road.'

'A farm?'

'He's cowman, sir.'

A cowman.

Gently said: 'Get in.'

3

Something else had come in during their absence from the police station: a message from the morgue. No grease had been found on the subject's throat, but such an abrasion as might have been caused by a finger-ring. Gently frowned over the scribbled note. He could remember no ring on Jackson's black paw. On the other hand, he had particularly noticed a cheap, silver skull-ring which the young fisherman had been wearing. But . . . Burrows?

'Did you talk to Mrs Burrows?'

'Yes sir.' Slatter pulled a face. 'Battle-axe is right. She stands as tall as me, and won't hear a word said against her son. Brought him up God-fearing, she did, unlike some she could name. If he says he was in by eleven, then in he was, and we can lay to that.'

'But did she see him come in?'

'Couldn't get her to say, sir. She jumped down my throat when I asked her.'

'So?'

'I'd say she didn't, sir. Only you're never going to get her to admit it.'

'Meanwhile, he didn't spend the evening in The Mariners.'

He told Slatter what he had learned there. Slatter listened, eager-eyed, registering each point.

'So ten to one he was chummie in the gateway.'

'Somehow, we shall have to make him speak up.'

Slatter looked doubtful. 'He's scared stiff of his ma, sir, and having met her I can't say I blame him.'

'We shall need a handle.'

Slatter's eyes were wicked.

'We know someone who scares him as much as his ma.'

Gently hunched. 'Perhaps. Or perhaps we shan't need him when we've talked to this brother.'

'The roughie who smelt of cow-dung, sir.'

'That's what we're going to find out.'

They waited; it was half an hour later when a patrol car parked outside, and a dishevelled figure, wearing handcuffs, was dragged from it and hustled in. Bartram tapped on the office door.

'We've had a bit of trouble with this one, sir,' he said. 'We can do him for an assault on an officer if you've nothing else in mind.'

'Just wheel him in.'

He still had to be dragged, red-faced, struggling, hair hanging over his face. About thirty, hefty build, wearing wellies and army-surplus fatigues: and Shavers had told no lies. The fellow niffed to high heaven of cow-dung.

'Sit him down.'

The two constables attached to him slammed him down on a chair with small ceremony. One of them had a bruised cheek, the other a fast-swelling lip. The man was panting hard, but for the moment had ceased to struggle: perhaps feeling that he had made his point. He sat glaring from under his hair.

'What's his name?'

'Henry Gillings, sir. He wasn't too keen on coming to the station. We had a bit of a chase through the cow-sheds. Didn't have any option but the cuffs.'

'He knew why he was wanted?'

'Yes sir, we told him. It was then he cut loose.'

'Did he make any answers?'

'No sir. Nor he hasn't said a word since.'

Gently regarded the odorous cowman.

'So what was the reason for all this, Gillings?'

Gillings glared back. 'Lousy pigs! Think they can do what they like, don't they?'

'You were asked here to help with our inquiries.'

'Suppose I never wanted to come?'

'Why would that be?'

'Bloody because! Get me here and I've had it, haven't I?'

'Is that a confession?'

'No it isn't.'

'You can tell us something about last night?'

'You get lost.'

Slatter murmured: 'Perhaps we should cool him off in the cell, sir.'

Instead, Gently pointed to the handcuffs. There was a moment of reluctance on the part of the constables: then one of them produced a key, and the handcuffs were removed. Gillings massaged his wrists.

'Lousy pigs!'

'Why didn't you want to come here, Gillings?'

'Because I was mucking out, wasn't I? Why should I come here on their bloody say-so?'

'You know what happened here last night, don't you?'

'I was mucking out, that's what. Then this pair of sods turn up and want to haul me away to a police station.'

'You don't want to help us?'

'It's a free country. What right had they got to haul me away? I got my job, work to do. Whose going to muck out the rest of the stalls?'

Gently said: 'We've been talking to your sister.'

'What do I care about that?'

But he'd stopped chafing his wrists, and the eyes behind the hair were watchful.

Gently said: 'She was having trouble with her husband.'

'Every bugger had trouble with him.'

'You knew about that, didn't you?'

'So why is that a reason to pull me off work?'

'Because you were going to do something about it.'

'She told you that?'

'She told us.'

'I'll be having a word with her too, the rotten bitch. It's the last time I do anything for her.'

'Are you denying you came to look for Barnby?'

'Yes, a lot of time I'd have to do that! When I've seen them bedded down it's time for kip, I have to get up again at five. So when am I looking for him?'

'Where were you last night?'

'Along with the cows, like I'm saying. And then a bite to eat and into kip – I have to be up when some of you lot are still snoring.'

One of the constables said: 'He lives in a caravan, sir. We called there first to look for him. It stands alongside the cow-byre, a good half mile from the farm. He lives alone there.'

'Lousy pigs!'

'Does he have a car?'

'An old Rover 2000, sir.'

'How far is his caravan from the village?'

'A couple of miles along a byroad, sir.'

Gillings snarled: 'You lousy lot! You're going to drop me in this, aren't you? I never set eyes on her old man last night, nor I was never away from the cows.'

Gently spoke: 'Is there anyone to speak for you?'

'I can speak for myself, can't I?'

'Someone to testify that you were at home?'

'Oh yes. Just ask the bloody cows.'

'You attended to the cows, had a meal and went to bed.'

'Now you tell me that I didn't.'

Gently said: 'I think you were in The Mariners last night.'

The eyes seemed to retreat further behind the tangled hair.

'Who says I was there?'

He had made a dash at the hair, but still it tumbled down over his brow. Sweat was glinting on leathern features that now were no longer flushed. And the smell of dung was more penetrating than ever. Or was it the smell of fear?

'I want a lawyer. You're trying to fix me. I've got a right to ring a lawyer, haven't I? I knew from the start what the little game was, as soon as I saw those pigs pull up. Well it won't work, I'm not going to have it. Just because I'm living out there on my own.'

Gently said: 'You were in The Mariners. You called for a pint and drank up quickly. You were in Harford last night. You had come there to look for your brother-in-law.'

'But it's Monica's word against bloody mine!'

'Not that you bought a pint in The Mariners.'

'That was another night –'

Gently shook his head. 'Last night. On the word of the man who drew you the pint.'

'So if I was there for a quick pint!'

'You were looking for Barnby, but he wasn't in there. He wasn't at home either. So where did you go when you left The Mariners?'

'I went home.'

'Without checking the other pub?'

'All right, I may have looked in there too.'

'And if he wasn't at home, wasn't in the pubs, wouldn't you know where to start looking after that?'

'Oh, you sod.' He was breathing hard again. 'I was only going to sort him out, wasn't I? Nothing like doing the bugger in, just keeping him away from Monica's kids. Monica was scared he was going to take them, cart them off to his sister's in London. He'd been hanging about in his car outside the school, she was worried stiff what he might do.'

'You meant to have it out with him.'

'Yes – like that.'

'To give him a beating to make him desist.'

'All right.'

'But then you got carried away, decided to end the threat for ever.'

'No.' He slammed down with his fists. 'I never saw him last night, did I? Not in the pubs, not at his house, not up at Beattie Lound's neither. He was in there all right, his car was outside, only I didn't want to bust in on her. And I couldn't hang about there all night on the off-chance he was coming out. So I buggered off home, didn't I? Like I said, I have to be up at five.'

'You were outside the house where he was later found strangled, and then you simply went home?'

'Yes, I tell you.'

'Your intent was to assault him, but you abandoned it, and went home?'

'Yes. Bloody yes. I went home.'

'Leaving your sister's dilemma unresolved?'

'I'd have seen him later.'

'But not last night.'

'I went home, I tell you. Bloody home.' And suddenly he looked up. 'I can prove it!'

'Prove what?'

'Prove I buggered off home. And another things hangs to it – if it wasn't me, then perhaps it's this other bloke you should be going after.'

Gently said: 'What other bloke?'

'Why, him that was there when I turned up. Him who saw me go off again. Him who I left outside the house.'

Gently said: 'You saw another man.'

'Yes.' Now there was excitement in the shadowed eyes. 'I almost bumped into him in the dark – coming across the playing-field, it was. So what about that? Least is he can tell you what time I cleared off – around ten, I reckon it was. I came back over the field to fetch my car.'

Gently said: 'Let's take this in stages. When do you say you arrived in Harford?'

'Be after eight o'clock, wouldn't it. After I'd seen them bedded down. I went to Luke's house in Harbour Road, but it was dark, nobody there. So then I looked in at The Mariners, and after that The Eel's Foot.'

'Did you ask after him?'

'Would you have done, if you were there to sort him out? I knew where to look, like you said, if he wasn't at home or wasn't in the pubs.'

'Where were you parked?'

'Back of The Eel.'

'Go on.'

'So I'm crossing the field, aren't I. And I run into this bloke at the far gate, where it's in among the trees. Just standing there he was. I happened to see him against the light from the house.'

'Did you speak to him?'

'Why should I? But he was watching the place, like me. And he was still there half an hour later, when I gave up and came away. Me, I reckoned he was one of her fancies, keeping an eye on her and Luke.'

'Can you describe him?'

'It was dark, wasn't it? He was tall as me, or taller. And he stood there quiet as a mouse. I never heard him move once.'

'Where were you?'

'Down the road. Just across from the gate.'

'Between nine-thirty and ten?'

'Near enough. Could have been there sooner.'

'Tell me what you saw.'

'Well – bloody nothing. It was black as the Devil's nutting-bag. I could see a light on downstairs and another one in the hall, and then there were lights back in the village. But you couldn't see nothing else.'

'Was the window curtained?'

'Couldn't see that either. It was a window at the side of the house.'

'What did you hear?'

'Heard her laughing didn't I? But I couldn't hear nothing said.'

'But you heard their voices.'

'Well, now and then.' He hesitated. 'Seemed to be argufying. Bloody Luke droning away, then she saying something, and laughing. Last I couldn't hear any more, save for an old owl up in the woods.'

'An argument.'

'That's what I thought. And then they went quiet.'

'Go on.'

'So I hung on some more, and then give it up and come away. Reckoned he wouldn't be out there just yet, and it was way past my time for kip.'

'You came across the playing-field.'

'I told you.'

'And this man was still standing where you first saw him?'

'Listen, I'm not making the bugger up! I could see him this time against the lights in the village.'

'So describe him.'

'I can't can I. Just his bloody head and shoulders against the lights. A tall bloke, taller than me, I couldn't see any more than that.'

'You passed by how close to him?'

'It's all the same. I only know what I'm telling you. The first time I nearly ran into him, going back I kept clear.'

'And you made no remark to him?'

'Why should I? He was there on the same lark as me. I thought good luck to the bastard, perhaps he'd hang one on Lukey for me.'

Gently stared hard at Gillings.

'You own a car.'

Gillings stared back. 'Why shouldn't I own one?'

'Did you buy it locally?'

'So if I did?'

'From Jackson's Garage?'

Gillings kept staring.

Gently said: 'A tall bloke, taller than you.'

Gillings' eyes were sharp. 'Are you saying it was Jacko?'

'I'm asking what you say.'

'It bloody could have been.' Gillings flicked at his hair. 'I'm not saying it was, mind, but it could have been. And then maybe he'd have known it was me. Are you going to ask him?'

Gently shrugged.

'Look, you've got to believe what I'm telling you! It's the truth, first and last. I never saw a glim of Lukey last night.'

Gently said: 'You left your car at a pub. Wouldn't someone have seen you when you collected it?'

His eyes were baffled. 'It was in the alley wasn't it? I don't know if any sod saw me. But you can ask, can't you?'

'We shall ask.'

'About ten it was. They hadn't turned out.'

'In the meantime, Gillings, you will remain in custody. Until we have checked your story.'

'But . . . what about the bloody mucking-out!'

'That will have to wait.'

For a moment it seemed he would explode afresh.

'You lousy pigs. You're going to have me, aren't you? And all I did was try to help my sister . . .'

Gently nodded to the constables. Gillings was removed. His smell did not depart with him. Gently motioned to the window; Slatter opened it. Gently lit his pipe, took lengthy puffs.

'So what do you think now, sir . . .' Slatter was beginning, when the phone rang, and Gently picked it up.

'Chiefy . . . ?'

'What do you want, Shavers?'

'Don't be like that, Chiefy! I've got something for you. Listen, there's this mate of Burrows, knows when he left the pub, where he was off to. It's what you wanted to know, isn't it?'

Yes: it was what Gently wanted to know. He pulled a pad across, selected one of Bartram's ballpens.

'Shoot.'

'A kid called Rushmere, comes from those cottages near the Castle – an oppo of Burrows he is, they're often in here together. So around half eight Burrows tells him he's off, the kid asks where, Burrows gives him a wink, says he's going to take a look at Beattie and particularly doesn't want any company. Then he scapa's.'

'At half-past eight.'

'Give or take five minutes, Chiefy. But you can't really believe it was Burrows?'

Gently hung up, finished scribbling, and shoved the pad across to Slatter.

'Put someone on this.'

He puffed some more while Slatter was transmitting the order. Slatter returned with a glint in his eye.

'We must get something out of this one, sir! If we can nail Burrows as the chummie in the gateway, I reckon he'll sing like a canary.'

'But what will the tune be?'

'I'm fancying Gillings, sir. We don't have anything solid on Jackson. And the way Gillings went for those two men, I can see him doing the job on Barnby. Motive too, sir, to finish him off – then Barnby's property will go to the sister. I'd say it was going through Gillings' mind when he was setting about Barnby.'

'But if Gillings was telling us the truth?'

'There's still Jackson, sir. Maybe Burrows caught a look at him.'

'And just maybe it wasn't Burrows in the gateway.'

'Shall I have him fetched, sir?'

'Have him fetched.'

About Gillings, one thing was certain: on his finger, a plain gold ring.

Gently went to stare through the window, at the square; the gapers who avoided his eye. One factor that was baffling him about this village tragedy was the level of violence that had been employed. A phenomenal level: he had seen victims before who displayed the classical injuries of strangulation, but none like this. If Barnby had been garrotted, the bruising could not have been more savage. Also, he'd appeared to have no secondary injuries, meaning that there hadn't been a fight. So . . . ? It seemed the man they were seeking was one of a strength well-nigh superhuman, a man-gorilla. Jackson? Gillings? Both were powerful men . . . but?

As for Burrows!

Then was there yet a fourth man, more strong, more determined than any of these – a fourth lover, who, it had to follow, had the protection, if not the connivance, of his mistress?

Unconsciously he shivered, staring out at the peaceful square, where buildings drowsed in the soft sun and shadows were growing longer. Something uncanny in this lonely village by its lonely river, on a lonely coast . . .

'Sir – trouble! We let Spratt go, and he's been spreading the tale about Jackson. Now half the village is out there, and Jackson is asking for protection.'

'Have you men there?'

'We've sent a car, but someone has just thrown a brick . . .'

Gently sighed. 'Let's go, then!'

'Sir, it's Mrs Burrows. I had a feeling that we might have trouble with her.'

'Half the village' was an overstatement, but quite a crowd had gathered on the road opposite the garage: mostly women, with a few men and youths hanging on. Prominent was a tall, elderly woman, with a hard, long-featured face; and supporting her a shorter, younger woman with dark hair and angry eyes. In the forecourt, two uniform men. At the office window, the frightened face of the pump-attendant. Then there was a brick lying on the bonnet of a car with a shattered windscreen. Deliberately, Gently swung fast on to the forecourt and halted with a squeak of tyres. He got out.

'Who threw that brick?'

A murmur, a stir among the crowd. One of the constables muttered apologetically:

'It happened before we got here, sir.'

'It did, did it?'

He stared at the crowd, then turned on his heel and marched to the office. The white-faced pump-attendant shrank from him as he pushed open the door.

'Did you see who threw the brick?'

Shakily she pointed to a youth in the crowd.

'Do you know his name?'

'Matthew Warren . . . he owed Mr Jackson for repairs.'

Gently marched out, beckoned a constable, marched across to where the youth was standing.

'Matthew Warren?'

The youth gaped.

'I'm arresting you, Warren, for criminal damage. You will accompany this officer to the police station.'

'But I never . . .'

'You let him be!'

It was the hard-faced woman who had interrupted.

'Take him,' Gently said to the constable. The constable grabbed the youth's arm, pushed him, half-ran him, to a parked Panda car.

'Oh yes, big men, big men!' the woman screamed. 'You're good at frightening the kids, aren't you? But what about him in there – when are you going to lay hold of him?'

'Mrs Burrows?'

'Never mind who I am!'

'My advice to you is to go home, madam.' Gently stared at the others. 'And that applies to the rest of you. Just depart quietly about your business.'

'And what about him?'

'Yes – what about him!'

It was the angry-eyed woman who had thrust forward.

'And what about my brother – you've got him, haven't you? But the bloke who did it – oh no!'

'You are Mrs Barnby?'

'Yes I am. I should think I've a right to be here, haven't I?'

'I would advise you to leave, madam.'

'Oh no. Not till I see that sod put away.'

'You can do no good here.'

'No good, he says. And him trying to hang it on my brother! When the whole village can tell you who did it – him in there, who daren't come out to face us.'

'You may be sure we shall pursue our enquiries.'

'Their enquiries!' Mrs Burrows screamed. 'Scaring a God-fearing boy like my Markie, trying to bully him into telling lies.'

'Why don't you arrest him – we aren't none of us safe.'

'Why don't some of you men go in for him!'

'Hold it,' Gently said. 'I can understand your impatience, but I repeat my advice, you will do well to go home.'

'Not till you arrest him!'

'Unless you take my advice, I may be forced to make charges.'

'Oh yes, that's easy, isn't it? So why aren't you making charges against him?'

Gently let his eye run over the gathering, fixing it on every last one. Then he turned and walked slowly across the road and the forecourt and into the barn. Boos followed him. He stared around him. A figure in overalls came cautiously from behind the car that stood over the pit. Jackson had a large wrench in his hand. He was sweating under his grime.

'You can put that down.'

'The bastards. They're working up to lynch me, aren't they.'

'You asked for protection.'

'I bloody need it!'

He was shaking: he kept the wrench in his hand.

'I think perhaps you had better come with us.'

'No!'

'It may be the only way to stop a riot.'

'But I'm bloody innocent.'

'Nonetheless. It's the best protection I can offer.'

'I won't be arrested. It'll be the same. They'll be round the police station if I'm there.'

'Do you have any relatives?'

'Not here I don't.'

'Perhaps we can find you a safe haven.'

He stared at Gently.

'They'll wreck this place.'

'We shall maintain a presence here.'

Outside the booing continued.

'Well?'

'Can I change my bloody clothes?'

'Is there a back way through to the bungalow?'

'Oh God. They hate me, don't they?'

There was a back way. Gently waited while Jackson scrubbed himself, donned a suit. Still they could hear the booing without, still Jackson was on the tremble.

'Have I got to go out there . . . ?'

'We'll soon have you away.'

They returned through the gloomy workshop. And then the booing broke into a crescendo, into a hissing: fists were raised.

'Just get me out of this!'

Gently hustled him across the forecourt to the Rover. Someone threw a clod of earth: it missed Jackson, struck the car.

'You stay!' Gently jerked to Slatter, then he was in the car, gunning the engine. He swept out of the forecourt, past jeering faces. More clods thumped the departing car.

'Lock me up. Just lock me up!'

They were out of range, were round the corner.

'All right, I did it . . . lock me up.'

'Is that a confession?'

'Bloody yes.'

'I'm asking you again.'

'Oh, for Chrissake. Anything you want, but lock me up!'

Gently drove fast to the police station, shepherded Jackson into reception. Bartram gave the garageman a shrewd look before cocking an eye at Gently.

'Comic goings-on, sir?'

'I want him away. In some quiet place outside the village.'

'Banged-up, sir?'

'If he gives trouble! For now, just somewhere out of the heat.'

Bartram said: 'I think I know the place, sir . . .'

Jackson had slumped on a chair. He was sobbing.

4

They got him away.

Bartram knew of a police widow who lived in a cottage on the back road of Thwaite; Jackson was whisked off there in a Panda car, and not a moment too soon. The crowd who had been laying siege to the garage quickly made their appearance in the square, so that Bartram was obliged to go out and advise them that the garageman had been taken elsewhere. Jeering, hissing, and a red-faced Bartram. Also Mrs Barnby, clamouring to see her brother.

'Don't tell me you haven't got him in there – he wouldn't leave his cows half mucked-out.'

'He is assisting us, ma'am –'

'We know what that means, and I want to see him – you let me in.'

'Yes – let her in!'

'I've got a right, haven't I? It was my old man who was strangled?'

Slatter slunk back a few minutes later.

'I've locked up and left a man there, sir. But everyone took off down to the village. I saw the pump-attendant back to her house.'

'What's happened to the man you sent to fetch Burrows?'

Bartram said: 'He called in, sir. He couldn't find anyone at the house, so now he's gone down to the yard.'

Gently stared for a moment at the mob.

'Ask Mrs Burrows to kindly step in.'

An indignant figure, she stalked into the police station and was ushered to the office. And outside the mob went quiet, as though suddenly bereft of a leader.

'Are you going to run me in, now?'

She had more the mien of a man than a woman. Near seventy, bushy grey hair, shabby black coat over a shabby dress.

'We wish to speak to your son, Mrs Burrows.'

'Oh no you don't. You've got him who did it. So you can just let Markie be, the idea of him being mixed up in this.'

'Where shall we find him?'

'Let him be, you hear me? You've played all the games you're going to with him. Then there's Monica's brother, that's a laugh, as though she hadn't enough to put up with already.'

'Do you know where your son is?'

'Minding his business. And the pity is you aren't minding yours.'

'I'm afraid we must speak to him.'

'Then you'd best find him. He had his lunch and went out. So you go and look.'

Gently shrugged, said: 'Last night. Were you still up when your son returned home?'

'Why shouldn't I be up? He's a God-fearing boy, never comes in later than eleven.'

'Then you had gone to bed?'

'Who says I'd gone to bed?'

'Is your son in possession of a key?'

'And that's no business of yours either, going about all sneaky, trying to prove that Markie's a liar. He was brought up proper, you understand? Reads his Bible, I see to that. And no truck with shameless women, let alone that daughter of Satan on the top road. There's plenty that do for you to pick from, so just you leave my Markie alone.'

'In fact he has a key. He let himself in.'

'That's what you're saying. Not me.'

'Does he have a key?'

'He was was in by eleven. That's what he's saying and that's the truth.'

'But you can't confirm that.'

'As God is his witness – and mine too, for matter of that.'

Gently slowly nodded. Mrs Burrows eyed him.

'Suppose now you tell us where we can find him?'

'Can't.'

'Would that be won't?'

'Just let him be is what I'm telling you.'

Gently nodded again. 'Thank you, Mrs Burrows. On your way out, would you ask Mrs Barnby to step this way?'

She paused suspiciously, then tossed grey locks, turned and stalked from the office. They saw her speak to Mrs Barnby, with the mob gathered round, and the latter's face turning up anxiously.

'The old bitch!' Slatter murmured. 'She knows where the kid is all right, sir. Knows what he gets up to, too, for all she let's on he's pure as snow.'

Then Mrs Barnby: more nervous now, single in the office with the two policemen. A pert face already showing lines, though she could be little over thirty; sturdy in a simple two-piece, blouse, and navy coat.

'Do I get to see him, then?'

'Perhaps later, Mrs Barnby.'

'But I've got to get back because of the kids . . .'

And suddenly the starch was going out of her.

'Please sit down.'

Slatter shoved a chair under her. She sobbed and dabbed with a child's handkerchief. It was almost a peep-show for those on the square, who were crowding together at the best view-point.

'Henry's all I've got left now . . .'

Presumably her parents and children didn't count.

'Not that I had much of a life before . . .'

She swallowed, blew her nose loudly.

Gently said: 'You are referring to your husband.'

'He was a pig. I can tell you that.'

'It may be that this wasn't his first transgression.'

'A pig. He was after the others from the start.' She sniffed. 'He was older than me. I knew he'd been around of course. He used to go after Beattie when she was single, but he had to lay off when she married Aaron. Aaron was a proper man, I can tell you. There wasn't any nonsense about him. Dear Beattie had to draw her horns in, and woe betide the man who lifted his eyes to her. The pity of it is he ever won that money, he didn't need it, he was doing all right. And now she's got it. It's the money, you know. That's the reason they run after Beattie.'

'You knew about the others?'

'Show me someone who doesn't. You can't live in a village, can you? It was going the rounds about Lukey before he'd been hanging his hat there a week.'

'And Jackson?'

'Jacko was a clever one, nobody suspected him till now. He could slip in there by the back way, and who was to say it wasn't a job on her car?'

'Your brother might also have slipped in the back way.'

'Oh no.' The dark eyes had fired up again. 'You can take this for gospel, mister, Henry would never run after a slag like her. Women don't interest him, that's a fact, and you can take it how you like. Just his old cows, alone out there. So you can stop getting ideas about Henry.'

'But . . . for the money?'

'Never mind the money. Henry wouldn't care about that either.'

'Yet he was there last night. Waiting for Barnby.'

'Yes, and you know why. Lukey wanted the kids, and threatened to have them, he's got a married sister living in Chingford. Henry came here to warn him off, and that's all there is about that.'

'To give him a beating.'

'All right then – he had to make the message stick. But he didn't come here to do him in, nothing was further from his mind.'

'But someone did him in.'

'Someone – yes.' A sudden doubt in the eyes. 'What's Henry been saying?'

'He has been helping us.'

'But what's he saying is what I want to know.'

'He certainly kept watch on that house last night.'

'Well he would, wouldn't he, if Lukey was in there?'

'With intent to assault him.'

She caught her breath. 'But he never did this . . . never.'

Gently said nothing. Mrs Barnby gazed at him, eyes fearful, lips quivering. A woman used to taking her own part. Now wondering if there was a part she dared play.

'I want to see him.'

Gently shook his head. 'I'm sorry, but you may not see him just now.'

'But you've got the one who did it – rotten Jacko. All the village knows but you.'

'Jackson is helping our enquiries.'

'Jacko did it. You aren't asking around. He had it in for Lukey over Beattie, they had a punch-up only last week.'

'He is helping us.'

'Then let Henry go!'

'Your brother is helping us also.'

'But he didn't – he wouldn't . . .'

There was no help for it: she burst into lavish tears again.

'I've got to get back to my kids . . .'

'We'll have a car take you home, Mrs Barnby.'

'Oh no you won't. I've got my bike. I don't want favours from the likes of you.'

She jumped up. Slatter opened the door for her. They saw her weeping outside, surrounded by the inquisitive. Then she made her way, weeping, towards the church, with Mrs Burrows and some others in attendance. And the rest separated into knots, stared a little uneasily, began to move further off.

Slatter said: 'She thinks he could have done it, sir.'

Gently grunted. 'We need Burrows.'

'The more I see of Jackson, sir, the less I like him.'

But it was Burrows who could be holding the key.

The phone rang: Gently took it; a DC Abbot reporting in.

'Sir, I've talked to this brother of the publican at The Eel's Foot. Him and his missus are staying at the pub and yesterday they drove into Wolmering. They've been parking their car in the alley at the back, and it was empty when they got back last night.'

'At what time was that?'

'About ten-thirty, sir. Just when the pub was turning out.'

'Was a car noticed there earlier?'

'Not by anyone I've spoken to, sir.'

And the phone again: a DC Cox.

'I'm in the call-box at the quay, sir. I've spoken to a fisherman who gave Burrows a hand to winch his boat down to the river.'

Gently smothered a curse. 'Which way did he go?'

'Towards Shinglebourne, sir. There's still an hour left of the flood.'

'Is there a boat we can use?'

'I can enquire, sir. But the man says Burrows will have to come down on the ebb. Says he hasn't got the power to stem it, though he may reach Shinglebourne before it changes.'

To chase him . . . or wait for him?

'Find me the number of The Mariners!'

Shavers' chirpy voice sounded excited, but Gently cut him short.

'Have you a tender for that yacht of yours?'

'Well yes, Chiefy –'

'Is it ready to go?'

It was: and Gently hung up on whatever else Shavers was trying to say.

'I was trying to tell you, Chiefy – it's about Jackson!'

He had briefed Slatter and left him to hold the fort at the police station: also he'd rung Shinglebourne and had a man dispatched to the moorings. Now he was striding, with Shavers scurrying alongside, to where Cox was already waiting on the quay.

'He was down in the village last night – it's the truth, but I'll bet he never told you. Him and his van. He dropped off a moped that he'd been repairing for Ivan Hicks. Ask Ivan . . . only he works in Sheepbridge, is on the late shift all this week . . .'

Gently growled: 'At what time was this?'

'Be seven or eight o'clock time, Chiefy. Only your men were round asking if we'd seen him, and Ivan can bust any alibi he's putting up . . .'

Gently shrugged – something or nothing! Jackson being economical with the truth. What it needed was a session with Burrows, and Burrows was somewhere up the river.

'Which is your boat?'

'The inflatable, Chiefy. You'll need me along, won't you?'

'Shove off and start that outboard.'

'Right away. She'll run rings round any fishing-boat.'

The inflatable was beached on sand by the quay. The engine, a big Mercury, fired second pull. Shavers held the boat up to the quay while first Gently, then Cox, dropped aboard it. Then they were away with a raucous burst, skimming over the wrinkled surface. Like magic, it seemed, the quay, the yard unwound, went by, began dropping astern.

'Who are we after, Chiefy?'

'Never mind!'

They were skidding by the upstream moorings: buoyed craft, head to current, most waiting their turn to be hauled up. Then followed shoaly, tidal banks, topped by marram grass and sere vegetation, sometimes receding into wide flats, split here and there by the winding drains. And the sun was down and, unless cloud supervened, mist would soon be rising . . .

'If we're after a fishing-boat, it's young Burrows. Are we out to bust him, Chiefy?'

'Do you know his boat?'

'All tar and patches – and the engine's a load of scrap. What time did he leave?'

Cox said: 'He'd have had a half-hour's start, sir.'

'With the tide under him.' Shavers was calculating. 'Could be at Friday's Yard by now.'

'When shall we be there?'

'Twenty minutes.'

But was Shinglebourne where the young fisherman was heading? Another four miles, with the tide still under him, and he would be running into Thwaite: and that way there were drains enough to conceal a small fleet of such boats. Meanwhile the light was fading and, far up the coast, the spark of a lighthouse was sharpening by the moment. A fool's errand? Even Shavers fell quiet as the empty reaches sped by.

Finally the stub of the Martello tower showed against a dusting of town lights: then the yacht club moorings, the club house, the sheds of Friday's Yard.

'Pull in to the yacht club!'

There a uniform man stood watching their progress with interest. Shavers slid the inflatable up to the quay-heading, Cox made a grab and held on.

'Any sign of our man?'

'Reckon he went by, sir. A lanky fellow in an old patched boat. Like he meant to pull in below there, but then he spotted me and kept going straight up.'

What was the use of swearing?

'How long since?'

'Be eight or ten minutes, sir.'

'Get on your set and tell them I want two men at Thwaite Quay – and this time under cover!'

'Yes sir. Sorry, sir.'

Abashed, the constable hauled out the aerial of his personal transmitter. To Shavers, Gently snapped:

'Get going, then.'

'But Chiefy, this is costing me petrol –'

'You'll be paid.'

'I've got my sodding pub to open –'

'I'll have a word with Myrtle when we get back.'

'Oh, sod everything!'

But the engine bellowed and the inflatable launched itself from the quay. Friday's Yard sped by and was lost behind a bend, and the filigree of town lights began to merge into mist. Ahead, the darkening river, drains, marshes, shoals that called for sweeping detours: four miles of water to fetch two by the map, and tricky going in full light.

'Have you lights?'

'Bleeding likely, isn't it? If I'd known I'd have brought the hand-lamp.'

'You know this stretch?'

'Going to find out, aren't we? And don't forget soon we're on a falling tide.'

In fact they'd run out of the flood and now were sliding over slack water: if they had the misfortune to run aground, they might well have problems in getting off again. But Shavers kept the inflatable travelling: clearly he did know that stretch of river. Against the misted pink panel of the western sky the long promontory hiding Thwaite was creeping towards them, black trees, the notched church-tower, long finger of stretching shoal.

Then Cox:

'Sir, I think I saw a boat!'

'Where?'

'Going round that bend . . . dead ahead, there.'

Gently snapped to Shavers: 'Can't we have more power?'

'It eats bleeding petrol . . .'

'Never mind that!'

Reluctantly, Shavers switched the throttle and the bows of the inflatable lifted. Now they were boring into the twilight at a speed that had to be reckless. But the bend swept towards them. The inflatable heeled, bumped several times in taking its new course. Then they could see it: perhaps quarter of a mile ahead: a black shape creeping over pale water.

'It must be him, sir.'

'Keep the speed on.'

There were several frustrating windings between them. On one they lost sight of the labouring fishing-boat as they had to stretch far out to clear the promontory. But then it appeared straight ahead, just open water separating the two craft.

'He's spotted us, sir.'

In the stern of the boat a tall figure had suddenly crouched; and clearly the boat was beginning to move faster, with more white water showing astern.

'So he wants a bleeding race . . .'

Contemptuously, Shavers aimed the inflatable at their quarry. They were coming up hand-over-fist, no chance whatever of the fishing-boat escaping them. Nor did it. While they had yet ground to make, it swung abruptly towards a low turf bank; and as it struck, the tall figure jumped out and sploshed across flooded grass towards higher ground.

'The cheeky bastard!'

They could only watch. The figure vanished into gorses that clothed a low knoll, into the dusk; and it seemed like an age before Shavers spun the inflatable alongside the bank.

'See if you can spot him.'

The unlucky Cox went sploshing across the bank in his turn, also to vanish: they could hear him calling Burrows' name, but calling with an interrogative note. He loomed up again on the bank.

'Sorry sir . . . I'm afraid he's away. You can't see a lot up there, and there's cover in all directions.'

'Isn't there a road over there?'

'Yes sir. I couldn't see him on the road.'

'Right. Get in his boat and stay there.'

'The boat . . . ?'

'We don't want him taking off in it again!'

It was galling. A few hours since and Burrows had been in their hands: only then they hadn't known that his information might be so critical. And now he was dodging them, doubtless egged on by the 'battle-axe', his mother – and his own fear of what he must admit to, and of it coming to her ears. Or . . . could there be more to it than that?

Gently stared down at the ancient fishing-boat, its many repairs, its rusting furniture, the bilge that had settled above the floorboards aft.

Might not Burrows, too, have nourished ambitions that one day the Lound fortune could be his?

'So what now, Chiefy?'

'Set a course for Thwaite.'

'But Chiefy, I've got to get this boat back!'

'I'll talk to Myrtle about your expenses.'

Shavers spun the engine to life again.

It was quarter of an hour later and full dark when they climbed the rungs at Thwaite Quay – to be promptly grabbed by two uniform men, who suddenly materialised at the spot.

'Sorry sir – thought you might be chummie!'

'I'll use the radio in your car.'

On the radio he ordered a detail to the area of search, at the same time swearing under his breath. A fool's errand! If he had simply waited, Burrows would probably have slunk home again, while now, turned into a fugitive, he might evade the police for days.

'Chiefy, I've got to get back . . .'

Shavers stood shivering by the car.

'What's behind there – where Burrows took off?'

'Just sodding fields and a few trees.'

'Houses?'

'There's a cottage where one of your coppers used to live.'

'A copper . . . ?'

'Now his widow lives there.'

It had to be Bartram's 'safe house'. Perhaps not a sanctuary for Burrows – but police widows were commonly observant souls.

'Get in.'

With the crew in the back and Shavers beside him, he wheeled the patrol car off the quay. It was a short drive down the winding back road to the spot where other cars were already collecting. Bartram came to his window.

'A rum old job, sir! His ma is doing her top back there.'

'That police widow. What is her name?'

'Mrs Goodrum. Lives another half mile up the road.'

Gently closed his window and drove on, past uniform men shining torches. The white walls of a cottage glimmered in his lights: he pulled over and parked by the gate.

'Wait for me.'

'Chiefy, Myrtle will skin me . . . !'

Ignoring Shavers, he went through the gate. Light glowed behind leaded windows where the curtains were not yet pulled. He knocked: the door was answered by a plump, grey-haired lady. Behind her lurked a shrinking figure with scared eyes: the garageman.

'Police. May I come in?'

'Is something going on? I saw a couple of our cars drive by.'

'Half an hour earlier, did a man go past here?'

'A tall young fellow in a tan slop?'

'It was young Burrows.' Jackson struck in. 'Running like a hare. Why are you after him?'

'Which way was he running?'

'Towards Harford,' the woman said. 'But I couldn't be certain who it was.'

'May I use your phone?'

At the police station Slatter was sounding flurried: in the background Gently could hear a familiar yelping voice.

'That damned woman! Someone must have told her you were chasing her son up the river. Now she's here raising Cain, threatening prosecution if we lay a finger on him.'

'Listen. I'm at Mrs Goodrum's. She's seen Burrows heading back towards the village. Have you any men there?'

'Abbot and Haynes.'

'Send them to cover the back road. Then raise Bartram on the RT and tell him to work back this way. Warn Abbot and Haynes to stay out of sight.'

'Yes sir. This chummie is getting to be troublesome.'

'If he reaches the village we may lose him again – his mother may have some other tricks.'

He hung up. Jackson had been following the conversation with narrowed eyes: now he edged closer.

'So what's he done – why is he running, and you chasing him?'

'You find that interesting?'

'Yes, I do! He was hanging round Beattie's, and you know it.'

'I know it. And so do you.'

'And what is that supposed to mean?'

Gently said: 'I've been listening to a little bird who says you weren't at the garage all yesterday evening.'

Jackson backed off. 'And I'm saying I was.'

'The little bird says you were in the village.'

'But I wasn't . . .' His gritty face had paled. 'Listen, I was doing a clutch on Bill Cooper's Volks.'

'You made a delivery in the village.'

'A delivery . . . but that was before tea!'

'Nearer eight o'clock I'm told.'

'That's a lie. It couldn't have been much after six.'

'But you did make that delivery.'

Jackson was gazing with baffled, fearful eyes. Mrs Goodrum, who'd moved a little down the hall, threw him a curious, appraising glance.

'Suppose I did?'

'Then you weren't in the garage.'

'But it was only dropping off a moped. I went straight back and got on with the Volks. I couldn't have been away twenty minutes.'

'Which you forgot to tell us about this morning.'

'All right then, I did.'

'So was that the only thing you forgot?'

'Yes – I'm telling you.'

'From your garage to Mrs Lound's house can't be more than half a mile.'

'Oh, you bastard.'

The hands, still grey, showed pale at the knuckles. Jackson's eyes switched past Gently, as though measuring a chance of a rush for the door.

'It's me you're after, isn't it? Just like those swine back in the village. You'll be their hero, you. You'll have your picture all over the paper.'

'I think you could help us.'

'I have bloody helped you. All I know about it I've told you. Ask Beattie. Just ask Beattie! I was never round there on a Sunday night. And as for fancying my chances with her, Lukey may have done, but not me.'

'With Barnby out of the way –'

'Ask Beattie. She'll tell you it was never on with us.'

'A lot was at stake there.'

'Oh, bloody hell. Leave me alone – and ask Beattie!'

He jerked away from Gently, pushed past Mrs Goodrum and vanished into the parlour. Mrs Goodrum made a face, then asked anxiously:

'He's not under arrest, is he – nothing like that?'

Gently paused, shook his head. Mrs Goodrum moved closer, sank her voice.

'We've been having a talk in there, and he's been telling me all about it. And I don't know, the impression I'm getting is that he might be telling the truth. He's terribly upset.'

'Keep your ears open.'

'I wasn't a copper's wife for nothing.'

Back in the car, he briefed the men, then set out slowly along the narrow road. But if Burrows was still lurking there they caught no glimpse of him on the journey. Shavers was on pins the whole way.

'Couldn't we go just a little faster, Chiefy?'

And:

'Tomorrow I'll have to fetch my sodding boat back – I suppose there's no chance of a lift?'

Gently dropped him in the square, under the eyes of a few remaining gapers, then pressed on into the police station, where the ominous figure of Mrs Burrows awaited him. She was off her chair in a moment.

'What have you done with him? Where's Markie?'

And then, like Mrs Barnby, she burst into a tempest of tears.

5

'The lady in the case has been on the phone, sir.'

In the end he'd got rid of Mrs Burrows, persuading her to return home and to wait for her son there. He had sent a uniform man with her with instructions to maintain a presence: her tears had quickly been stemmed, but broke out again as she was leaving:

'He's an honest lad, Markie – why can't you let the poor boy be?'

'We will keep you informed, Mrs Burrows.'

'It's a crying shame . . . a crying shame!'

Then he had looked in on Gillings:

'When are you going to let me away?'

'We are still checking your account of last night.'

'Ah. But why can't I get back to my cows?'

And meanwhile time was marching on. And no word from Bartram and the detail.

'You have a man outside her house?'

'Just to stop her feeling lonely, sir. But now she's asking us to call him off, says she's getting obscene phone calls about him. Says there's enough of us around without a bobby outside her gate.'

They exchanged glances.

'Perhaps expecting a visitor?'

'I wouldn't know, sir,' Slatter said.

'Is her number handy?'

'On the pad, sir.'

Gently pulled the pad over and dialled.

'Mrs Lound?'

'Oh . . . it's you, is it?'

Harmonics suggested the scene: with her hand over the mouthpiece, she was saying to someone: 'It's *him*!'

'You have someone with you?'

'Oh, don't get stroppy! It's only Norah, who gives me a hand. What with last night and that corny copper, my gentlemen friends haven't been around.'

'Norah . . . ?'

'Norah Rivett. Her who you saw going off this morning. We're old friends, me and Norah, so I asked her over to keep me company. Any objections?'

'Is she all who you're expecting?'

'Lay off it, who'd be coming to visit me now? Even that copper turned me down when I invited him in for a drink, and then his old woman rang up and accused me of trying to seduce him. One of the snoopers out there must have told her. Thank gawd she only had one ten p.'

'Was hers the only call?'

'No it wasn't. When you rang just now I thought you were another. Bitchy women for the most part, along with a couple of heavy breathers. Can't you do something about it?'

Gently shrugged at Slatter. 'Were any of the calls threatening?'

'Only one from old mother Burrows. Said if I didn't stay away from her lilywhite son she'd be round here with the tar and feathers. Is it right that he's done a bunk?'

'Who told you that?'

'Norah.'

'We wish to talk to Mark Burrows.'

'Well, he isn't here. Though even a wet like him would be someone.' She paused. 'You're still on the job, then?'

'The investigation of course continues.'

'Do I get to see you again?'

'Have you something fresh to tell me?'

'Don't know, do I, till you start asking questions.'

Gently traded a further stare with Slatter.

'Perhaps you should come to the police station, Mrs Lound.'

'Oh, go on, it's not the same, is it. I should probably dry up if you had me in there. And maybe there are a few things you should know. Somehow, I can talk to you better than the others.'

'Suppose you tell me on the phone.'

'You come over here. I mean, I'm the one it's all about, aren't I?'

He hung up, and gave Slatter a resumé of the conversation. Slatter's mouth was twitching.

'Perhaps she really does know something she hasn't told us yet, sir . . .'

'If you were Burrows, where might you head for?'

Slatter's eyes sharpened. 'Burrows . . . yes. He would know we'd have him if he went home, while the lady might be persuaded to take him in.'

'I think that's certain.'

'He'd spot the man on the gate, sir.'

'If there's a back way, he would probably know it.'

'So we accept her invite?'

'I accept it. You carry on with business here.'

Slatter looked disappointed: also cautious.

'Don't think I'd go in there alone, sir.'

Gently nodded. 'My sentiments entirely. So I'll just borrow the WPC from the desk.'

The rear entrance of the police station gave access to a lane which led to the main gate of the playing-field, across which the fan of trees marked the position of the Lound house. Another dark night, with mist in addition, and not the smallest stir in the air. Beside Gently the WPC, a solid girl, did her best to match him step for step. Light from the house beckoned uncertainly: no watcher was loitering among the holm-oaks. In the road, the constable ceased his slow pacing when he heard the sound of their steps.

'All quiet?'

'Very quiet, sir. I was going to call in to see if I was still needed.'

'Hang on for a moment. Do you know Mark Burrows?'

'Yes sir. I'm local in the village.'

'We want him, and he may turn up here.'

'Right you are, sir. If I see him, I'll detain him.'

'Keep an eye on the garden too.'

They went through the wicket gate, and Gently rang. Almost

at once the porch-light was switched on. Then the small optic in the door shadowed, and finally came the rattle of a chain.

'Thought you'd take a chance on me, did you?'

Behind Mrs Lound, the woman of the bicycle. She was gazing at Gently with rapt interest, but Mrs Lound was staring at the WPC.

'Did you have to bring her with you, then? I should think you're man enough on your own.'

'If we may come in, Mrs Lound.'

'Oh, make yourself at home . . . and my name's Beattie, didn't I tell you?'

She had changed her garb since the morning, now wore a sweater, skirt and black embroidered tights. The Rivett woman, a dowdy blonde, was also dressed in skirt and sweater.

'Norah, put some coffee on, there's a dear. Daren't offer this bloke anything stronger.'

She closed the door and put the chain on again before leading them through to the lounge.

'Park yourselves.'

The lounge was modestly lit by two wall lights. Curtains had not been pulled across the windows; but little was visible beyond the dark panes. From the garden, however, the room itself must have shown up like a stage set.

'Shall we pull the curtains?'

'What for? There's no one out there, unless it's your bloke. We never have to pull the curtains out here excepting those at the front.'

'Still . . . shall we pull them?'

After a pause she tossed her head, and went to pull them. Then she came back to the settee and curled herself on it like a cat. With two fingers she adjusted her skirt, at the same time leering at the WPC.

'She a friend of yours, or just standing in?'

'As I understood it, you had something to tell me.'

'Only said I might have, didn't I. And I didn't expect you'd bring her along. Playing safe, is it?'

'The officer is on duty.'

'Dare say she'd look better tarted-up. It's the uniform, isn't it? Those black-out stockings. What do they wear along with those?'

The WPC was on her feet.

'If it's all the same to you, sir, I'll wait outside!'

'Stay,' Gently said.

The WPC hesitated, sat down again, on the edge of her chair. She stared venomously at Mrs Lound; Mrs Lound smiled at her husband's photograph.

'Now,' Gently said. 'No games. Just remember we're here on serious business. A man died outside here last night, and the way he died wasn't a pretty one.'

Mrs Lound pouted. 'So you're the big man. You've been going through Harford like a dose of salts. You've got Jacko, maybe you'll get Markie. And then there's Lukey's brother-in-law sitting in the chokey.'

'Who told you about him?'

'Norah, who else? Why do you think I asked her round? She was up with the others, outside the garage. If you want all the news, ask Norah.'

'Is Gillings an acquaintance?'

'Have a heart. I just heard Lukey talking about him.'

'What did he say?'

'That he was a crude bastard who might cause trouble some time.' She fixed her brown stare on Gently. 'So why not pinch him? He must be in the running, or you wouldn't be holding him.'

'Do you know him by sight?'

'I've seen him around. Drives an old Rover that's half rust. I know that Lukey was worried about him. Said that blokes like him were often touched in the head.'

'Have you seen him lately?'

'Not to remember.'

'When was the last time?'

'Oh, I don't know! Last week. He was parked on the square. Glared at me as though I should have dropped dead.' She gave her throaty chuckle. 'Maybe he was on the lookout for Lukey then, I don't know. But he's a right so-and-so. I'll bet he isn't saying where he was last night.'

The brown eyes were sharp.

Gently said: 'If I wished to search this house, would you have any objection?'

'Do what?'

'Conduct a search.'

Now the eyes had gone very still.

'What are you getting at?'

'Perhaps the officer here could take a quick look round.'

'Oh bloody no! Not that sour bitch. She doesn't move out of this room.'

'Then you object to a search?'

'I didn't say that, did I? But I'm not having her prying around. If you want to go upstairs that's fine with me, call it a search or what you like. Is that the idea?'

'The idea is a search.'

'But what the hell do you expect to find?'

'Have I your permission?'

She stared long and hard. 'You're going to bloody do it anyway, aren't you?'

Gently stationed the WPC in the hall, which commanded the lower part of the house: then, with Mrs Lound dogging him close, he made a quick round of the ground floor rooms. They comprised a bleak dining-room, a second sitting-room, a breakfast-room, kitchen, scullery and cloak-room. In the kitchen the Rivett woman was setting cups on a tray: she paused to stare with intrigued eyes.

'What's outside?'

'Just the garage. And a shed.'

'May we look?'

'You can dig the garden if you like.'

In the garage, a Maestro with last year's date-letter; in the shed, lumber, gardening tools gathering rust.

'Now we'll go upstairs.'

She followed him silently as he climbed the thickly-carpeted stairs. A lavish bathroom, chilledly fragrant, and four bedrooms, three plainly unused. Then the fourth. It was at the front, with a bay window facing towards the village, and struck one at once with a warm, scented atmosphere. A deep carpet, a pink, circular bed, a dressing-table loaded with bottles, sprays; a huge white wardrobe, its door hanging open, two padded chairs with underwear draped over them. She gave a gurgling laugh.

'What do you think?'

'Be good enough to pull those curtains.'

Are you afraid your bloke down below may see us?'

'Just pull them.'

'Why not?'

She went to the window, gave a mocking wave, then swept some pink velvet curtains across it. Gently went to the wardrobe, ruffled through the contents. The bed was too low to offer concealment. Mrs Lound meanwhile had plumped down on the bed.

'You think I've got a bloke tucked away here, don't you?'

'Is there a loft?'

'Oh, give it up! You have to look, I don't care, but you needn't have brought Miss Sourpuss with you. We're friends, aren't we? So close the door. Let her stand in the hall and wish it was her.'

'We will go down.'

'But we've only just got here. You don't have to worry about Norah.'

'This way, please.'

'If I ripped my pants off and screamed bloody rape, where would you be then?'

Gently stood by the light-switch.

'You sod.'

But she bounced off the bed and brushed past him.

'Your French bit has spoiled you, that's it, isn't it? So you haven't got time for talent like me . . .'

The hatch to the loft was over the landing: had a festoon of cobweb across it.

'Is that the lot, then?'

They were back in the lounge, where the Rivett woman had fetched in the coffee. Now she was handing round the cups, the WPC getting one with a flooded saucer. Having handed them out, she hesitated, then took a seat near the door.

'I mean you haven't found anyone, have you, and that's the reason you came here. So now you can leave us in peace. There's a programme I want to see on the box.'

'You wish to get rid of us?'

'Oh no. I haven't seen enough of the police for one day. And you can take that copper outside with you, I've seen all I want of his ugly face.'

She drank meanly. She was still furious: the cup was quivering in her hand. She had barged against the WPC when entering, and the latter was nearly as furious as herself. All this the Rivett woman had watched with unconcealed glee.

'Who did you think it was anyway – who would I be likely to have out here? You've got your hands on Jacko already, and if it wasn't him you've got the other one. And I asked you out here, that's a laugh. Asked for bloody police protection.'

'We have to conduct checks.'

'Oh yes. Which means you can do what you like, doesn't it? Because shouldn't you have had a warrant when you came to search my house?'

'Your permission was sought.'

'My foot. I was conned, and you know it.'

Was she keeping her voice raised deliberately? It was probably quite audible in the garden, and perhaps to the constable on the road if he had remained close to the gate. Otherwise the house was silent: silent the night outside.

'A short time ago I was speaking to Jackson.'

'How nice for him. What did he say?'

'He referred me to you. He seemed to think that your testimony might exonerate him.'

'A fat chance of that.'

But her interest was aroused, and her stare now held curiosity. A moment later she drank up and put down her cup.

'I could twist Jacko round my finger, you know that? But I'll say this for him, he was never jealous. Just a great big lug who came when I called him, stayed clear when I didn't.'

'He would do what you asked him.'

'Don't get me wrong. I didn't need his help to hand Lukey his cards. I can look after my own affairs, and when I've done with a man, he knows it. No, Derek is just a softie. If that's what he meant you can hear me telling you.'

'A lover with no expectations.'

'A lover, I like that. And he got to first base, didn't he? With a little help though, I have to admit it.'

'Wouldn't he have formed expectations then?'

She tossed her head. 'He knew different. I don't have to marry, why should I? Why should any woman who's got it made? I didn't kid him, he knew from the start that we were just going to be good friends. Same with Lukey. Only Lukey thought he just needed to push that little bit harder.'

'And wouldn't that have troubled Jackson?'

'Well . . . it might have.'

'Perhaps you teased him?'

Her smile was strange. 'Perhaps.'

'So that, increasingly, it appeared to him that his relationship with you might be in jeopardy?'

The same smile.

'And then happened an incident, this violence between the two men, possibly convincing Jackson that Barnby was on the point of succeeding?'

'You've got it all worked out, haven't you?'

'It may have pushed Jackson over the edge. So that now his hope is that you will support him, will persuade me that nothing of the sort applied.'

'Aren't you the tricky one.'

'Well?'

'You've shut me up about Derek, haven't you? Now, whatever I say, it's because I'm trying to get him off.'

Gently said: 'Not Jackson.'

Mrs Lound didn't reply.

'And if we don't fancy Gillings either?'

Just for an instant, could there have been fear in the probing eyes?

'What are you trying to get at now?'

Gently shrugged. 'I would have thought that was plain. If not Jackson, if not Gillings, then we are seeking a third man.'

'A third man . . . you can't mean Markie?'

'Burrows appears to be a prospect.'

'You're crazy. He couldn't do it. Lukey gave him a hiding, don't you know that?'

'But if he had taken Barnby by surprise?'

'Him and who else. Lukey was tough. Markie is just a long streak, I could handle him myself.'

Gently said: 'Not Burrows.'

She swirled her red hair. 'I'm tired of this game!'

'Not Jackson. Not Gillings. Not Burrows.'

'Oh wrap up. So who are you saying?'

Gently said: 'We're looking for a big man. A man of exceptional physical strength. A man probably over six feet in height, massive build, huge hands. A man you should know. Who has been your lover. Who you have given reason to entertain expectations. Who may not now be living in the village, or even in the near vicinity.'

No doubt this time about the look in those eyes!

'But I don't know any bastard like that . . .'

'Such a man was the strangler of Luke Barnby.'

'I don't care. I don't know him . . . has he got a name, this marvellous bloke?'

'He wears a ring.'

'Oh Christ. Who doesn't?'

'I think you must know who I mean, Mrs Lound.'

'Wouldn't I have told you then?'

'Would you?'

'Yes, I'd have been the bloody first!'

Gently held her in a hard stare: she tossed her head, stared away. Then her eyes came back.

'You rotten devil. You've got Derek – what more do you want? So I don't want you to have him, why should I, I like to have that lug around. But if you want him, bloody have him, it's no skin off my nose. Sure he could have done it. Sure he wanted me, may have been after the money too – you've seen that mouldy outfit of his, it could stand a packet of Aaron's cash. Only don't expect me to put a noose round his neck. I owe the silly bastard that at least. And that's all you're getting out of me.' She laughed nervously. 'And give him my love the next time you see him.'

'You are willing for us to have Jackson.'

'If you want him. With bloody compliments.'

'Or Gillings.'

'Who you damn well like. If he fills the bills, you have him.'

'But not the man I described.'

'Oh, turn it in. He doesn't exist, and you know it. You've been asking around all day – if there was such a bloke, wouldn't you have heard of him?'

She jumped up, went over to the bar, splashed a drink into a tumbler: stood, a defiant figure, tipping back the raw gin. Now the WPC was watching her with an odd expression, almost of admiration. And the Rivett woman, who hadn't spoken a word, with a stupid simper on her face.

'So do I get to see my programme, or shall I dish out the booze to you too?'

'Who are you expecting here tonight?'

'It's the bloody truth, not a soul. Norah's sleeping here. Do you think I would have asked her if I'd something else in mind? I don't need help, I can tell you. So name your poison, if you're staying.'

She poured more gin. It seemed clearly her intention now to get sloshed. Or to pretend to: she sipped the second drink with more restraint than the first. She giggled.

'What a lot you look, sitting round there like so many images! The big man. I'll bet he isn't so fireproof when his gooseberry isn't about. And her, well get a drink in her and see what she's made of then. And Norah, my love – no tales, eh? But all of you sitting around like judges . . .'

Gently said: 'We shall certainly find him.'

'So bloody find him, what do I care?'

'Perhaps I should warn you, Mrs Lound, that you may be committing a serious offence.'

'Like hell I am. I don't know anything, and nothing is what you're getting from me. That's on the square, isn't it? So name your booze or get out.'

The Rivett woman said: 'I'll have a drink, Beattie –', but then the phone jangled in the hall. At once Mrs Lound stiffened, her eyes suddenly big.

'You take it, Norah.'

'Stay,' Gently said.

'But damn you, this is my bloody house!'

'Nevertheless, I must take that call.'

'Oh you bastard. And I thought you were decent.'

Glass in hand, she scuttled after him as he went out to the hall.

'Yes?'

It was only Bartram to say that the search had drawn a blank.

'So are you going or are you staying?'

They were back in that gloomy, tasteless lounge, the Rivett woman equipped with a drink, Mrs Lound embarking on her third. They had been there an hour. Had Burrows spotted the constable, or taken fright from the raised voice of Mrs Lound? Somewhere still, out there in the night, he must be wandering, denied a refuge.

He daren't go home, probably had small resources, by now would be hungry and cold. What remained for him but to hang about here, hoping they would go and leave the coast clear?

'I'll take that drink.'

'He's bloody human! This I never expected to see.'

'And one for my officer.'

'Go on. She'd choke before she took a drink from me.'

In a level voice the WPC said: 'Thank you. A small one.'

And small was what she got: a wet of gin.

Were they wasting their time? It had begun to look like it as the minutes ticked by. Some other option must have occurred to the fugitive: he perhaps had a bolt-hole of which they knew nothing. At the last sighting he'd been making for the village, but the men in wait had waited in vain. Had he taken to the fields, doubled back, outflanking the sweep of Bartram's detail? A foolish young man . . . or was he? Was there more to him than met the eye?

'Aaron should have been here to see this.'

'Aaron . . . ?'

'Bloody near teetotal, my old man. For five rotten years I had to hide the bottle, or make an excuse to nip into The Mariners. I mean, I was brought up to the stuff, not like I was a miss from a Sunday school. He should have married one of them, eh? Just plain badness, him picking on a barmaid.'

'Didn't his luck with the pools soften him?'

'Don't make me laugh . . . made him worse. The obstinate sod. And look where it got him. When they brought me the news I got soused for a week.' She gurgled. 'He'd be stone cold sober and singing a hymn when he went down. Men bloody men. I should tie up with one again.'

The Rivett woman said: 'You haven't lost time since, Beattie.'

Mrs Lound hiccupped. 'Six lovely years. But I still haven't got the taste out of my mouth . . . that's what a bloke like Aaron does for you. A rotten shame. Men. I've been taking it out of him ever since. Expectations with me, there aren't any, and you can write that down in your little book.'

She drank, and drank again: yet was it really that which was making her speech slur? Her eye was as lively as ever, watching to see how Gently would take her. Three gins, and now a fourth . . . but hadn't she been 'brought up to the stuff'?

'Think I'm hiding someone away . . . huh?'

She hadn't sat down, was leaning on the bar.

'But I'm telling you the truth, policeman. Isn't one of them stands a chance with me. So who is it, huh? This third man. A bloody secret he's got to be. Give me his name, may have heard of him, could be I screwed him when I was drunk. Got a name has he?' She wagged her head. 'No name. Because why? No man!'

Then the phone jangled again, and she was screaming:

'Let that bloody phone be!'

'Excuse me, Mrs Lound.'

'My home . . . my phone . . . !'

'See to her,' Gently jerked to the WPC.

He went through, slammed the door on the tumult developing behind him.

'Gently.'

Slatter's voice said: 'I'm afraid there's been a cock-up, sir . . .'

'A cock-up?'

'DC Cox, sir, who you left guarding Burrows' boat. Well, he'd got pretty wet, and when he heard that Burrows was heading back to Harford . . . well, he got a lift back here, sir, leaving the boat unguarded. But it turned out all right in the end, sir . . .'

'How do you mean, turned out all right?'

'We've got Burrows.'

'You've got him?'

'He just walked into The Mariners, sir. Seems he must have circled round the search party and gone back to his boat. Then he came down on the ebb, and the next thing I get a tinkle from Shavers.'

Gently took a long breath. 'What's he saying?'

'Acting the innocent, sir.'

'I'll be straight back.'

He hung up an instant before Mrs Lound burst through the door.

'I want to know who that call was from . . . !'

'It was a call for me, Mrs Lound.'

She glared at him in baffled fury, behind her a red-faced, ruffled WPC.

'You sod. You're playing games with me, aren't you?'

'Just continuing my enquiries.'

'You know what? You remind me of Aaron. And now I'm going to smash that bastard's picture.'

Outside, the hubbub must have attracted the notice of the constable, since they found him lurking close to the front door.

6

'That woman knows what she isn't telling, sir.'

They were striding back across the dark playing-field, the WPC bobbing beside Gently, the constable a couple of paces in the rear.

Beyond the village, somewhere at sea, throbbed the faint luminescence of a lightship, while the houses showed few lighted windows: a dark night at Harford was very dark.

'A man . . .'

'Yes sir. I felt certain of it. A man who wasn't Jackson or the other fellow.'

'Nor Burrows.'

'She was expecting him to ring, sir. That second time she was desperate. I had to pretty well fight her off, almost like it was a matter of life or death with her.'

'A man we aren't on to . . .'

'Yes sir. And like you said, not living in the village. She was near panic when you gave that description, it must be pretty close to the truth. Then after that she pretended to get drunk, though I daresay she was feeling in need of a drink.'

'Jackson, Gillings we could have.'

'Anyone to head us off this other man, sir.'

'Who she suspects, to put it no higher.'

'More than suspects would be my opinion.'

Gently shrugged to himself in the darkness – had Mrs Lound seen those injuries to Barnby? He had forgotten to ask, and the likelihood was that she'd been kept well away from the gruesome scene. But at least from a distance, say the bedroom window, she could have gained an idea of the horror. Careless, resistant of close ties with her men, would she yet seek to shield the author of that? It seemed unlikely: she'd stand at risk from the man, and equally at risk from the law.

As though reading his thoughts, the WPC said:

'There's usually one man with her sort of woman, sir. You see it with prostitutes and their protectors. They would do anything for that one man.'

'She isn't a prostitute.'

'She's that type, sir.'

Meanwhile, at the police station, Markie Burrows.

'The other woman, Rivett, may be worth a word with.'

'You'll be lucky to get anything out of her.'

It was as though night had thrown a switch on the village, on the square. The gapers had vanished to a man, and the only parked vehicles were police cars.

Harford didn't run to street lights: the few shops were shuttered and black. Lights showed at The Eel's Foot and behind one or two curtained windows, but most illumination came from the police station, because of which it had an isolated air.

'Has Mrs Burrows been informed?'

'No sir . . . I thought that could wait.'

'Send a man round. At the same time advise her that she can't see him yet.'

'She'll be round here, sir, in a flash.'

'Keep her well away from the office.'

He himself lowered the office blinds, though now there were no watchers outside. The office, too, was indifferently lit, a single bulb under a flat shade. He took his seat at the desk, pulled out his pipe and laid it before him.

'Bring him in.'

Slatter fetched the young man, who overtopped the Inspector by almost a head. Under the light he looked even more colourless, the sleek hair whitish, eyes frail. The legs of his jeans were still damp, damp socks showed above damp trainers. He stood helplessly before the desk, eyes lowered: like an animal awaiting disposal.

'Sit, then.'

'I ought to get home –'

'Your mother has been told you are here.'

'I wasn't doing anything –'

'Take that chair.'

'Checking my nets was all it was.'

Slatter nudged him with the chair and he sat clumsily, long legs sprawled. He had a spent air about him, doubtless occasioned by his exertions. On a thick finger, the skull ring. His hands were held gripping his thighs.

'Have you something to tell us?'

'I don't know! I never knew it was the police after me.'

'So why did you run away?'

'Well wouldn't you? I could see that someone was out to get me.'

'Policemen in uniform?'

'I never saw them, only three blokes in a rubber boat.'

'What made you think they were chasing you?'

'Well . . . after me like that. And all these things going on.'

'Things?'

'You know what I mean. I could have finished up like Lukey, couldn't I?'

'And you went up the river just to check your nets?'

'Going to check them coming down. Only then I couldn't.'

Was it possible he believed what he was saying? His hands were mechanically kneading his thighs. His head was drooped, eyes fixed on the floor between his feet. Gently said:

'Would you like to smoke?'

'Me? I've run out of rotten fags.'

Gently nodded to Slatter, who went to a drawer, took out a pack and proffered it to Burrows.

'Ta . . . thanks.'

Slatter found him a light. Burrows puffed nervously, then defiantly inhaled. Gently said:

'Now we'll start again. You didn't go up the river to check your nets. You went because you lied to us this morning, and knew we should find out that you had been lying.'

'No I never –'

'Wait. I'm going to read from a statement we have taken. It was made by one, Phillip Rushmere, who was in The Mariners with you last night.'

'But he doesn't know nothing –'

'Listen. He says he was drinking with you until half-past eight, then you said "I'm off now, I'm off to see Beattie", and he said, "Do you need any help?" You replied, "This is for the men, sonny," and after that you left.'

'He's a lousy liar!'

'You didn't leave?'

'Went to the loo. It was a joke.'

'You didn't leave The Mariners?'

'No I never. I come back into the saloon.'

'I have a verbal statement from another source that you were absent from The Mariners after that time.'

'I was there 'till closing.'

'That you bought two halves, and were not seen after you bought the second one.'

'I was there for half an hour –!' He floundered, the hands on the thighs working overtime. 'I'm going to have it out with Phil Rushmere, he hasn't got no right to tell lies about me.'

'You left half an hour after buying your second drink?'

'No, I never meant that . . . it was half an hour before I went to the loo.'

'Between eight and ten-thirty you bought no more drinks?'

'No . . . why should I, you don't have to.'

'And you have witnesses to prove you were there.'

He'd long forgotten to suck at the cigarette.

Gently said: 'At half-past eight you left the pub with the expressed intention of visiting Mrs Lound. In a gateway close to her house we find cigarette ends of the brand you smoke. On cigarette ends are traces of saliva. Saliva can be type-tested. The cigarette ends have been sent to a laboratory. I may also have to send the cigarette you are smoking.'

He goggled at Gently. It took time to sink in.

'You mean . . . my spit?'

Gently nodded.

'You can't do that!'

'We can do it.'

'Bloody can't.'

'We can prove, beyond doubt, whether you were at that spot last night.'

'Not like this you can't.'

And suddenly he was ripping the butt from the cigarette, jamming it into his mouth and masticating like a madman. Gently watched the performance unmoved. Finally Burrows managed to swallow the butt. Then he reached forward to stub the remains of the fag in the ashtray on the desk.

'So what about that, then?'

'We can still sample your saliva.'

'No you can't. If I won't wear it.'

'If you refuse a request for a sample we shall have to assume that your saliva is a match.'

'But you won't know, will you?'

'The assumption will stand. If given in evidence in a court of law.'

'But look . . . it's all stupid! Because I'm not the bloke you want, am I?'

Gently shrugged, picked up his pipe, stuck it empty in his mouth and drew a few times.

'You have been Mrs Lound's lover, haven't you?'

Even here he felt he had to glance over his shoulder.

'No. It isn't true.'

'Though we have her word for it?'

'She didn't mean that . . . it was fixing a shelf for her.'

'That isn't what she says.'

'I tell you, no!'

'For some time you have been infatuated with her. You spend much of your time loitering in that gateway, hoping that what had happened once might happen again. You saw Barnby entertained there. Jackson. You knew that Mrs Lound didn't take you seriously. But still you kept going. You were there last night. You saw Barnby's car, but you didn't go away.'

'You can't prove none of it!'

'There was a light on downstairs, perhaps one in the bedroom too. Then the bedroom light went out, and still you waited in that gateway. She wasn't taking you seriously, what could you do, how prove to her that she was wrong? In the end you waited till Barnby came out, the door had closed, the porch-light was switched off.'

'But I was in The Mariners – I was!'

'In court, we can prove different.'

'I was home before eleven, my ma will say so.'

'Your mother will stop short at an outright lie.'

'Oh dear, it isn't what you're saying. I never saw Lukey last night at all. And I was never there.'

'You were frequently there.'

'No . . .'

At which point, a commotion out in reception.

'He's here – and I'm going to see him!'

A babble of voices, Bartram's the loudest!

'Don't you dare lay hands on a woman – I'll have the law on you, just you see!'

'If you'll wait here, ma'am –'

'Don't madam me. I know my rights, and I'm going to see him.'

'Just now he's helping –'

'Helping, is it? Just let me through . . . I'll do some helping!'

The effect on Burrows had been electric. At the first sound of her voice he had shot up from his chair. Now he was pressed against the wall of the office, as far as possible from the door.

'Please . . . don't let her come in here!'

'You do not wish to see your mother?'

'No – please. Not now. I never knew she was coming round here.'

'She has been concerned about you.'

'Oh, please. If she finds out . . .'

Still empty pipe in mouth, Gently rose and went through to reception. At once a clamour from Mrs Burrows:

'Let me through! What are you doing to him in there?'

The WPC was hanging on to her, Bartram was barring the way to the office: Cox, Abbot and a uniform man were clustering round to lend assistance.

'Take your hands off me, you bitch!'

Gently gestured. 'Let her go.'

'She's been trying to force her way in, sir.'

'I think she understands we must ask her to wait.'

Reluctantly the WPC complied, and Mrs Burrows shook herself, shook her wild locks. She planted herself in front of Gently, fixed a fierce eye on his.

'What have you done to him – go on, tell me! I know he's been hunted high and low.'

Gently said: 'Your son is unharmed. In the end we found him in The Mariners.'

'He was up the river – that I know!'

'He came down again on the ebb. He gave no trouble. At the moment he is assisting the enquiry.'

'He's here – so I'm going to see him.'

'You will see him a little later.'

'I'll see him now! Markie – Markie – it's your mother. Come out here!'

But Markie didn't come out there. Gently said:

'He expressed a wish that you should wait.'

'That's likely, isn't it? My own son. Why wouldn't he want to see me now?'

'If you will take a seat.'

'I don't want a seat! I want to see what you're doing to Markie. Putting lies in his mouth, that I'm sure of, making him say whatever suits you.'

'It will be best if you are patient.'

But patient she was not for several minutes. However, the outbursts at last subsided, and then one could see that she was trembling. She accepted the seat; Bartram sent the uniform man to brew tea; finally Mrs Burrows sat grimly silent, eyes fixed on the office door. Bartram murmured:

'I was near enough to getting my face worked over there, sir!'

Gently grunted, went back into the office, shut the door carefully behind him. Burrows was still hugging the wall. His pale eyes were large on Gently.

'She – she can't hear us?'

'She can't hear us.'

'And you . . . you wouldn't have to tell her?'

Gently shook his head, sat again at the desk, slowly began to fill his pipe. The young fisherman crept back to his chair and, when he sat, sat on the edge.

'It's true, then.'

'What is true?'

'I'd do anything for Beattie.'

Gently lit his pipe.

'Go on.'

'It isn't the same – like you think.'

'Not the same?'

'I mean, as just fancying her.' He gulped. 'I'd marry Beattie, if I could. She's more than – you know! More than people think she is. All those others. It's just a laugh with them. And Jacko and Lukey. But I love Beattie.'

'A woman so much older than yourself?'

'I can't help it. She was kind to me. I was in love with her before that, but when it happened . . . she was kind. Like I meant something, wasn't just another one. Like I'd got my feelings too. She knew I never had . . . Ma doesn't like me going with girls.'

Gently blew smoke rings. 'So?'

He glanced to the door. 'I had to keep it dark, didn't I? Ma's religious, got this thing, scarlet women and all that. Don't know what she'd do if she found out I was going with Beattie. I'm her only son now, see. My brothers got drowned off a drifter.'

'Your mother must know you hang about there.'

'I tell her it's football, don't I.'

'But after dark?'

'She doesn't know. I can go to the pub, she'll wear that.'

'When in fact you are up there?'

'I can't help it. I've just got to see Beattie sometimes.'

'And at the same time keep an eye on the others.'

He hung his head, stared at the floor.

Gently said: 'Admit it. You were jealous.'

His head came up. 'Well, it wasn't fair! They were having everything, him and Lukey, when all the time it was me . . .'

'And Lukey caught you.'

'Thought I was spying on him, going to tell on him to his missus. It was after that . . . but he never knew. It was once after he had gone.'

'Jealous. You wanted to supplant them.'

'They didn't care. Just using her, weren't they. It was me

who loved her, not them. All they were after was her money.'

'But not you.'

'No!'

'The thought of her money didn't come into it.'

The pale face was tormented. 'I don't know! Perhaps, a bit. But it didn't matter. I never thought about the money, just . . . Well, all I've got is my old boat.'

'Nothing to offer her.'

'Ma . . .'

He didn't need to finish the sentence.

Gently puffed. 'Now we'll get to last night!'

Burrows' hands were busy again. Under the one light his lank pale hair looked almost like a cap on the longish skull. The head jerked.

'Because of Norah, wasn't it?'

'Norah?'

'She does for Beattie on a Monday.'

'So?'

'Well . . . I reckoned she wouldn't have a bloke staying on there. Not with Norah turning up in the morning.'

'You thought that?'

'It was a Sunday before, like. Lukey cleared off early then. So I thought . . . well, I thought it might be worth me having a try.'

At another time the naivety would have been touching.

'You left The Mariners at half-past eight.'

'Yes. About.'

'You went up through the village and across the playing-field and took up a stand in the gateway.'

He just nodded.

'Did you meet anyone?'

'I saw some blokes outside The Eel's Foot. And I could see a bobby in here. Across the field it was too dark.'

'When you got there you saw Barnby's car.'

Another nod.

'What else.'

'Like you said. There was a light on in the bedroom. Then it went out. And I could see one downstairs.'

'So you waited.'

'I went home –'

'You waited. Lit a cigarette.'

'I tell you –!'

'Two cigarettes.'

'Look, I just wasn't there when Lukey came out! I had to go, it had got late, she'd have given me a mobbing if I'd stayed any longer. There was another bloke came and had a look and then cleared off. But he could have come back. And then I thought I saw –'

'Hold it,' Gently said. 'What other bloke?'

'I don't know! I don't think he saw me, but he was there all right, outside her gate. You've got to believe me.'

'Another man.'

'He came over the field. I was stood right back in the holm-oaks. Went past close he did, but he didn't act as though he'd seen me. Went to look at the car. Then he hung on a bit, maybe it was twenty minutes. And then he came back past me and cleared off towards the village.'

'A man known to you.'

'No. Only he was there, I'll swear on a Bible.'

'What time did he arrive?'

'I must have been there an hour, half-past nine or something after.'

'Can you describe him?'

'Dark, wasn't it.'

'As tall as you?'

'No he wasn't.'

'Nothing you can tell me about him?'

Like a drowning man he clutched it:

'He smelt of cows.'

'He smelt of cows.'

Gently struck a fresh light for a pipe that had gone out. Burrows was staring helplessly, unable to divine if he were being believed. At Gently's elbow, Slatter had leaned back, was surveying the young man with an intrigued expression. From reception, no sound: as though there they might be holding their breath. Gently blew smoke.

'He went. You stayed. Tell me what happened then.'

'I tell you, nothing. And I didn't stay –'

'Until the time the pubs turned out, you stayed.'

'I was home by eleven!'

'Let's say after.'

He swallowed. 'Wasn't much after. I daren't stay after eleven. She heard me come in as it was, shouted down to know what time it was.'

'What time was it?'

'Eleven I told her. She may have switched on the light to see. Maybe ten minutes, quarter-past. But I was away from there at eleven.'

'From after half-past eight till eleven you were watching outside that house.'

'Look, that other bloke could have come back –'

'Try to remember anything you saw.'

'But it was dark, wasn't it?'

'There were lights in the house.'

'Yes, well. I could see when they went on and off. They were in the bedroom when I got there. Then they were downstairs in her sitting-room.'

'When the other man was there?'

'Yes. Before that. I could see him trying to squint in, but the window's at the side. He couldn't see anything.'

'He didn't go through the gate.'

'No he didn't.'

'Would you say that the curtains had been pulled at that window?'

'I couldn't see that. All I could see was some light shining out on the bushes, like.'

'On the bushes.'

'Look, I was going to tell you. I thought I saw old Lukey come out for a moment. He didn't stay, though, just went back in. I thought that perhaps he was on his way.'

'You saw him where?'

'Well, at the side, like. Where the light was coming through the window.'

'Barnby.'

'Yes. He came out for a moment. I could see his legs. Then he moved away.'

'You heard the door open and close?'

'Didn't hear nothing. I just saw him, that's all.'

'The legs of a man.'

'It was him, not Beattie.'

'Barnby.'

'Had to be Lukey, didn't it?'

Gently puffed a few times.

'Was this before or after the other man came?'

'After, it was. Must have been near eleven, which was why I thought Lukey was on his way. Only he wasn't, he went back in, and I knew it wasn't much use me waiting any longer.'

'You saw no more of him.'

'No, I swear it. He was still in there when I left.'

'Heard nothing. Saw nothing.'

'It's the truth. I came away down, and that's all I know.'

And ten to one he'd seen Barnby's killer. Or at the least, seen the killer's legs.

Gently said: 'Right, Burrows. What I want from you now is a written statement. I want you to write down all you have just told me. The Inspector here will give you a hand.'

'But – you aren't going to tell on me? About Beattie?'

'You can leave that part out of your statement!'

'But you won't let on?'

'What tale you tell your mother is your own affair.'

In reception he brushed Mrs Burrows aside, beckoned Bartram to the counter.

'Any further confirmation on Gillings?'

'Yes sir. One of my men turned in a report. His car was seen parked where he says it was at around half-past eight last night.'

'He's off the hook. Unless you want to charge him.'

Bartram rolled beefy shoulders.

'Reckon it's all in a day's work, sir. And I'd sooner have his smell out of here.'

At the phone, Gently raked off Mrs Lound's number: her voice sounded markedly the worse for gin.

'You bastards again! Can't you leave us in peace? One would think it was me who did for Lukey . . .'

'A query about last night, Mrs Lound.'

'Sod last night. I've had last night.'

'At any time, after he arrived there, did Barnby go outside?'

'It's where you found him, isn't it? Or are you saying he was done in here?'

'Meaning between the time he arrived and the time he left.'

'Well, he didn't come here to pee on the flowers.'

'He didn't go outside?'

'Why should he?'

'He didn't.'

'No. Now for creeping jesus . . .'

Gently hung up. Then Mrs Burrows:

'I'll take the book in my hand . . . he was in bed by eleven!'

And getting towards eleven it was again by the time the young fisherman had signed his statement, had been delivered to his mother, and the pair of them were driven home. A day's work: with a glimpse at the end of it, just a glimpse, of the chummie they were after; one suspect eliminated, one on the file, and a witness who went home half an hour too soon. Wearily, Gently sank into the Rover and set out to drive the empty roads, past trees that lit pinkish or yellow in his headlights, through villages deserted and dark.

At Heatherings he drove straight to the garage and was getting out to open the door: but then light spilled from the front of the house, and Gabrielle came running across the gravel.

'My dear, your people are on the phone – urgently, they wish to speak to you!'

Oh did they!

He still paused to kiss her before going to take the call in the hall.

'Gently here.'

'Sir, you'll hardly believe this, but we've got another stiff on our hands.'

'Another what?'

'Another stiff, sir. And this time it's Jackson.'

'Jackson!'

'The same like before, sir. And we were there only minutes after it happened. Mrs Lound rang us to say he'd turned up, but by the time we arrived he was dead. And listen to this, sir. We've made an arrest. We picked up Burrows at the scene.'

'Burrows . . .'

'Yes sir. He's swearing his head off, but he was there. And Jackson is dead.'

Gently said flatly: 'I'll be straight back.'

Poor Gabrielle!

Her eyes said it all.

He hadn't the heart to get back in the car before he'd added an embrace to that perfunctory kiss.

7

Was it merely tiredness that afflicted him as he drove back along those crooked roads, or was it veritable, that sensation of malevolence abroad in the misty night? Not a car passed him, not a light was showing, no life in hamlet or field: no owl caught suddenly in his headlights, no deer come clattering out of the forest. A dead of night that had never seemed deader or more remote from the things of day: vacated. And in the vacuum this sensation of evil, of terror.

As he drove the last narrow miles he could see ahead the throbbing lumination of the hidden sea-mark. A dull pallor pulsing like a nerve, it seemed to body and point the sensation he felt. Out there the sea, and by the sea the village: stricken, fearful, and alone. An evil from that way? From the stones of the castle? From some unimaginable, terrifying past?

But finally his headlights lit the deserted garage, all windows dark, its pumps forlorn, and found the junction of the minor road that led to the flashpoint of the trauma. And here there were lights, cars, men, an ambulance waiting, flash-bulbs fizzing. He jammed the Rover in behind the ambulance.

'Where's Burrows?'

'Took him in, sir.'

'What's his story?'

'Say there's a bloke ran away and drove off in a car.'

'How soon were you here?'

'Pretty well at once, sir.'

'Any sighting of a car?'

'No sir.'

And the body was still hanging over the gate, with a couple

of hand-lamps playing on it. With Slatter in attendance, Gently went over, stared at the very-dead garageman. His hands hung down, still seamed with grease. His clothes, the suit Gently had seen him pulling on. Same injuries to the neck. And, oddly, the cuffs of his trousers tucked into his socks. But then, a bicycle, a lady's model, was lying in the hedge by the gate.

'What excuse did he give Mrs Goodrum?'

'Said he wanted to fetch his night-things, sir. She says you told her he wasn't under arrest, so she lent him her bike to ride over here on.'

'Mrs Lound rang you?'

'Yes sir. Said Jackson was there making a nuisance of himself. She'd been talking to him with the door on the chain, but he wouldn't go away and she wanted him picked up. So we got over here fast, only it wasn't fast enough. There he was, slung over the gate, and Burrows we copped coming over the playing-field. Couldn't have been more than minutes after.'

'And no sign of any other person.'

'No sir. Just Burrows. And the ladies were inside, never knew what had happened.'

'Get him away.'

Bartram signed to the ambulance crew, who were standing by with a rolled stretcher. They made a mess of getting Jackson off the gate and the body lumped to the ground, still soft. One of them tried to close the staring eyes, but they crept open again, even after two attempts. On the stretcher you could see the neck injuries plainly and they included the mark, perhaps made with a finger ring. He was covered and dispatched. In the house, lights. But no face peering from a window.

'Who is in there?'

'WPC Joyce, sir. The lady's in a state, you can imagine.'

'Where does Burrows say the car was parked?'

'Down by the junction.'

'See if you can find any indications.'

The wicket-gate creaked as he and Slatter went through; it was the WPC who answered Gently's ring.

'She's been drinking again, sir . . .'

Gently shrugged, went on through to the lounge.

'Can we have more lights . . . ?'

'Bugger the lights!'

Mrs Lound's face was sweating and distraught. She was sitting on the settee, but bolt upright, an empty glass in her hand. Mrs Rivett also had a glass, was looking pale. She was sitting in one of the outsize chairs. There was a standard lamp: Gently switched it on. Better lit, the room looked yet more vulgar.

'So what now, you bastards – how many more?'

'Hush, Mrs Lound,' the WPC said.

Mrs Lound's eyes flashed. 'Go screw yourself, Maggie! Where's it going to stop, that's what I want to know – how many more is this sod going to do for?'

Gently said: 'You rang the police station after a conversation with Jackson.'

'I bloody did – and where did that get me? You bastards couldn't catch a cold in a draught.'

'What time did he arrive here?'

'How should I know?'

Slatter said: 'The call was timed at eleven twenty-two, sir.'

'So then he was here at quarter-past – with Dracula outside waiting for him.'

'You saw a second person?'

'Did I hell. I never took the chain off the door. I wanted bonzo in here, didn't I, him who like as not did for Lukey.'

'So what was his purpose here?'

'Shit-scared, wasn't he? Wanted me to swear this and that. Said you'd believe me if I told you he was innocent and never gave a damn about Lukey. What a laugh.'

'And that was all?'

'Said I should have stuck to him, wouldn't have been any trouble at all. Said now maybe we could hit it off together if I stood by him. Bloody men.'

'It would have been plain to a bystander that he was a lover.'

'So what. When was that a secret.'

'From the conversation it was plain.'

'I'm telling you aren't I? Told him straight out he'd had his last screw with me.'

'But still he wouldn't leave.'

'I was getting scared, wasn't I. The sod wouldn't take no for an answer. I mean he could have broken in. So I slammed the door and went straight to ring you lot.'

'After that you heard nothing?'

'Heard the gate creak, like he might have taken off.'

'When was that?'

'While I was ringing.'

'And nothing else?'

'Bloody nothing else.'

She threw her glass at the hearth, where it shattered on the tiles. She was trembling, sweating profoundly. It darkened the armpits of the sweater, glinted in the creases of her neck.

'So what now, what now?'

Gently said: 'It might be best if you spent the rest of the night elsewhere. Perhaps at The Mariners.'

'Oh bloody no. Not with Myrtle and Chick I don't.'

'Then with a friend.'

'What rotten friend? A fat lot of those I've got round here. No, I'm not budging.'

'It might be safer.'

'Yes, and leave you lot to snout round everywhere. You're going to be here, aren't you?'

'We shall certainly be here.'

'All you big strong men, then! And it isn't me he's after, anyway, so you can forget about turning me out.' She shook hair lank with sweat. 'It's bloody wonderful. He slips through your fingers just like that. Or are you on to him?'

Gently said nothing.

'Bloody Dracula I mean! Are you or aren't you?'

'We are pursuing enquiries.'

'You aren't going to tell me, is that it?'

'We have certain information.'

'Bastard.'

For an instant her eyes were fierce. Then she jumped off the settee, brushed past him to the bar, poured gin into a fresh glass.

'So you've got what you came for – now naff off. And take little Miss Maggie with you.'

'You have nothing more to tell me?'

'Naff off! This is my house, and I want you out of it.'

'First I intend to check through it.'

He thought she would throw the glass at him. But then she burst into tipsy laughter and collapsed on the settee, slopping the gin.

'Naff off – naff off – naff off!'

'Stay here,' Gently said to the WPC. With Slatter he made a quick round of the house, checked windows and doors, sent Slatter to the garage.

'Was the garden searched?'

'Yes sir.'

In the lounge, Mrs Lound was still gurgling to herself. All this time the Rivett woman had sat stiffly, not speaking a word. Gently asked her:

'Can you add anything?'

'It's like she said. They talked through the door.'

'Did you see anyone?'

'No fear. I was back down the hall, out of the way.'

'You heard me describe the man we are after. Do you know one who might answer the description?'

'Oh gawd, no. Nobody in Harford. Nor nobody I've ever seen here.'

'Put the chain on the door when we leave.'

They went, taking the relieved WPC with them. Outside, Bartram said:

'Up the road, sir. Some tyre marks on the verge, and a spot of oil.'

'Could they be recent?'

'Hard to say, sir. We haven't had rain for some days.'

'What time was Gillings dropped at his caravan?'

'Around eleven, sir . . . do you want him checked?'

'I want him checked. And tell the man to feel the engine of Gilling's car.'

Fewer lights outside the house now: the photographs were taken, the body gone. Men who had spread out to search the area were returning to the cars, standing around. The urgent moment slowly subsiding, the dark night closing back in: by daylight a fresh search, but now what could be done was done. And still that sensation of a brooding evil, of violence let loose: as black as the night.

'Do we know how Burrows managed to dodge his mother?'

He could just see the snatch of Slatter's head. 'She's down there, of course! Seems like he told her he moored his boat in a hurry, would have to slip out and adjust his lines.'

'Instead of which he came here.'

'I reckon he was lucky, sir. Might have been him and not Jackson. Supposing he isn't chummie, and his neck is sticking out. I'm not sure I can swallow the tale he tells.'

'Another lover . . .'

Because now they were certain. The killing of Jackson was quite impersonal. At the wrong place at the wrong time, and they could finish up decorating Beattie Lound's gate.

'First what I want to know is what you were doing outside the house.'

In the eyes that faced him across Bartram's desk was a fear that could not be hidden.

They had run the gauntlet in reception, and in fact Mrs Burrows seemed a good deal subdued. Grabbing Gently's arm imploringly, she had exclaimed:

'What are you going to do with him?'

'There has been a fresh incident . . .'

'I know – I heard! Another one gone to meet his Maker. And him that everyone thought . . . but you can't be thinking it was Markie.'

'We need your son's account.'

'He's a decent lad!'

'I must ask you again to be patient.'

'He never had a father . . . but I brought him up . . .'

The WPC had come to Gently's assistance.

In the office a uniform man had been planted before the door; and indeed the young fisherman gave the impression of being ready to bolt. Jammed down on a chair by the constable, he sat crouched, as though ready for a spring. And the hands which formerly had clutched his legs now were clutching the edge of the seat.

'I w-wanted . . . I felt I had to . . .'

'This was getting towards midnight.'

'No – just after eleven. Just after the car took us home.'

'At that time of night, what were you doing there?'

'I-I wanted . . . I felt that she . . .'

'That she wanted to see you?'

'Yes! I didn't know . . .'

'At that time of night?'

'Well . . .'

He stared desperately at the dead-eyed Slatter, at the desk. At the floor.

'I . . .'

'Yes?'

'There was only me left, like. And she was up there all alone. I felt . . . well, if I could just tell her there was someone she could depend on . . .'

'You didn't think your appearance might alarm her?'

'No – why? It was only me.'

'You, who were there last night as well?'

'But I wasn't . . . I mean! She couldn't ever have thought . . .'

'Twice you were there. Twice a man has died.'

'But I never was . . .'

'Twice. First Barnby, now Jackson. Two obstacles in the path of your wooing.'

'I only went there because . . .'

'Because you thought she needed you.'

'Please, yes! It's the truth.'

And the look in the pale eyes was so pitiful that you were almost compelled to believe him.

'Very well then. You lied to your mother. You took yourself off to Mrs Lound's house. Half an hour later you were picked up. Let's hear what happened in between.'

'I don't know what happened . . .'

'From the beginning.'

'Only I never . . .' He swallowed. 'So when I got there he was just riding up. I saw him shove his bike in the hedge.'

'Jackson.'

'I didn't know it was him, not till I heard him talking to her. He went up and rung the bell, and then she opened the door a bit.'

'You heard what was said?'

'Yes, some of it. I didn't like to go too close – got the porch-light on, she had, they'd have seen me if I'd gone out there.'

'You were in the playing-field gateway.'

'I never shifted out of it. I tell you, he rode up as I got there. He'd have seen me by the light of his bike. I kept back behind the holm-oaks.'

'What did you hear said?'

'She was mobbing him wasn't she, said he'd got to eff off and she was calling the police. And he was begging her to let him come in, said she was the only one who could save him now. Said she must know who it was who'd done it, anyway she knew it wasn't him.'

'Jackson said she must know who had done it?'

'Yes, going on about it all the time. And she said he was balmy and she'd done with him, and she was going to ring the police and have him picked up.'

'The light was on in the porch.'

'Yes, I told you.'

'You could see Jackson, Mrs Lound, the gate.'

'Yes, I had to keep back –'

'You saw no one else.'

'No . . . not then.' He swallowed again.

'Go on.'

'Well, she slammed the door, didn't she, and him still shouting for her to let him come in. So then he gave up and come away, and I backed off so he shouldn't see me.'

'You backed off.'

'Behind the holm-oaks.'

'You could no longer see Jackson or the gate of the house.'

'It's the truth, I went back behind there, or he'd have seen me when he put on his light.'

'Only he didn't put it on.'

'No! And I kept waiting for him to go. Like I knew he hadn't, because . . .' Fear was back in the pale eyes.

'What was it you heard?'

'I don't know! I never guessed . . . not right then. Like it might have been a tussle he was having with the bike, got it stuck in the hedge or something.'

'You heard no cry.'

'No . . . nothing. The way I said. A sort of tussle with something.' He dragged on the chair. 'And me wishing he'd get on with it, clear out, leave me to have a word . . .'

'You didn't go to see what was holding him up.'

'Oh lord no, I never. Just waited for him to go, switch on his light, clear off.'

'And then?'

'See the bloke, didn't I. See him run past and down the road. Her light was still on, I could see him a bit, a huge great bloke. Bigger than me.'

'Bigger than you.'

'Bigger. Huge great head, got a beard I think.'

'Could you see his clothes.'

'Couldn't see them. Just his shape. Then he was gone.'

'You didn't hear his voice.'

'Just him running down the road. Next I heard a car door slam, the engine starting. Then his lights as he drove off. After that . . .' He shuddered. 'I came out and had a look.'

'You saw Jackson.'

He nodded.

'Then?'

'Oh lord.' He covered his face. 'It was like Lukey must have been. Over the gate. Like a rug hung out.'

'Did you approach him?'

A snatch of his head. 'See him there in the light. When I saw the bloke run I'd begun to guess. I never went nearer than across the road.'

'So?'

'Just wanted to get away from there.'

'It didn't occur to you that Jackson might not be dead?'

'Had to be dead. Knew it. All I wanted was to get away.'

'You ran.'

'I don't know. Next thing I was being grabbed. I tried to tell them, they wouldn't listen to me, said I was making the bloke up.'

'And you weren't making him up?'

'No. I swear it!'

Gently said: 'Last evening you were in The Mariners. A man such as you describe was a fellow customer. Couldn't it have been him who gave you the idea?'

'I never saw no one like him in The Mariners!'

'A big man with a beard. Off a yacht.'

'Oh – him.'

'Then you do remember?'

'But this one was bigger – like I'm telling you.'

'You could tell me any size. Because only you saw him.'

'Look, it's true, all what I've been saying.'

'There was such a man.'

'Yes. Him that run away and drove off in a car.'

'A man bigger than you.'

'Yes.'

'Bigger than the yachtsman in the pub.'

'Yes – I reckon. Bigger than him.'

'But no other description.'

'Look, it's true . . .'

And it had better be! Wearily, Gently reached for the phone to put out an alert. But by now that very large bearded man, if he existed, could have gone to earth or be fifty miles off. Burrows watched with agonised eyes.

'It's true . . . and I didn't make him up . . .'

'Tomorrow I shall need another statement from you. Just for the moment, get out of here.'

'Then – it's all right?'

'Take him out!'

But just then came a tap on the door. Entered a constable minus his head-gear and with an eye beginning to discolour.

'Sir . . .'

Gently gazed at him. 'Don't tell me – you've brought in Gillings.'

'Yes sir. We felt the engine of his car.'

'And it was warm?'

'I'd call it hot, sir.'

It was like a re-run: smell and all. The manacled Gillings was hustled into the office. Struggling, protesting about lousy pigs, he was thrust down on a chair.

'I'm going to write to my MP or some bugger . . . !'

He hadn't come off scatheless, either. On his grainy jaw was a fresh weal, in the grubby fatigues, a rent.

'If we take the cuffs off will you behave?'

'Lousy pigs. Lousy bastards!'

'If you want to spend the night in a cell –'

'Buggering people around. It isn't right.'

But once more, having made his point, he calmed down and held out the manacled wrists. Then resentfully worked his freed hands, his narrowed grey eyes squinting at Gently.

'You sods are going to keep after me, aren't you?'

'Don't you think we have some reason?'

'That bastard was mucking about with my car, so I clouted him one. Who wouldn't?'

'I'm not referring to that.'

'So what?'

'Where did you go in your car tonight?'

'In my car? That's my bloody business, no cause for you pigs to drag me back here.'

'We drove you to your caravan. That would have been at about eleven. After that you went out in your car.'

'So if I did. Paid my tax, haven't I? Bloody MOT too, and that cost me a packet.'

'You drove back to Harford.'

'Likely, isn't it.'

'You parked your car at a certain spot.'

'Oh ah. Right outside here.'

'Are you denying this?'

'Bloody my business, isn't it?'

'It happens to be ours too, Gillings. Which is why you are sitting on that chair. And either you tell us what we want to know or you finish up in a cell.'

In the flickering eyes, genuine incomprehension: and thin lips were gapped over yellow teeth.

'Look . . . what's it got to do with you buggers if I was driving around all night?'

'Do you tell us, or not?'

'But why should I?'

Gently drilled him with a stare.

'Oh blast it, then. If you must know. Drove round to Mo Jermy's, didn't I?'

'Mo Jermy's?'

'Ah, Mo's. On account of being sodded about by you lot. Need a hand in the morning, don't I, and Mo was the only one I could depend on.'

'You spoke to this man?'

'Tried to, didn't I.'

'Only tried?'

'The bugger wasn't in. Then I remembered he was away for the weekend, got a day or two off to visit his sister.'

'So you spoke to no one.'

'W'no. He took the missus and kids with him, didn't he?'

'In fact, you can't prove you were not in Harford?'

'But I bloody wasn't. I was at Mo's.'

Gently said: 'We think you were here. We think you were parked near Mrs Lound's house. We think you were seen running away from the house. We think you may have had some reason to run.'

The gapped mouth.

'But, bloody hell! I never came back here, why should I?'

'Didn't come back here?'

'No I never. I drove to Mo's, like I said.'

'We need proof of that.'

'But Mo wasn't there.'

'And, going and coming, you met no one?'

'Blast, at that time of night? There was only this bugger who nearly smashed into me.'

Gently said: 'A man in a car?'

'Ah. As I was turning outside Mo's. Going like the clappers he was, a bit pissed it wouldn't surprise me.'

'A man in a car.'

'I'm telling you.'

'Did you catch sight of him?'

'Ah. A big bugger.'

'Anything else?'

'Got a bloody great beard and driving a red car, don't ask me what.'

'A big man with a beard driving very fast.'

'Ah. And the sod bloody near clipped me.'

Gently said: 'Fetch a map.'

A map was spread over the desk. Not without difficulty,

Gillings identified the minor road where the incident occurred. It connected the village with the main north-south road that paralleled the line of the coast. The driver had been heading in the direction of that road. By now, could be anywhere in the eastern counties.

'Can you estimate the time when this happened?'

'Oh ah. Half-eleven time, say.'

Which fitted.

'A saloon or a hatchback?'

'Yes, I was noticing things like that!'

For the rest, Gillings was a dry well: but what he'd given them was enough. This man existed, was no more a hypothesis, and reports from patrols might throw light on his whereabouts. The information was fed through. Gillings, feeling the pressure off him, followed this procedure with naïve enthusiasm.

'Is this one the bloke, then?'

'We wish to question him.'

'Ah. And that's saying he is, like, isn't it? And don't forget he bloody near had me too, he's a sodding menace in a car.'

'You may go, Mr Gillings. We will drive you home.'

'All this buggering-about is his doing.'

Gillings went: it was 2.00 a.m. Bartram brought in mugs of strong, sweet coffee. Now all was silent in reception, outside no cars were leaving or returning: 2.00 a.m. And somewhere a man, a man beginning to take shape, a man with two stranglings already on his conscience: out there in the darkness, the beleaguered night. Also, it might be, not far away: within simple driving-time of the house up yonder.

Slatter mused: 'She has to know who he is, sir.'

Probably. But she wasn't saying.

'It stands to reason.'

Yes. But if so, she wasn't going to give him up: yet.

'Tomorrow, all stops out. We have to find him.'

'Yes sir. We'll check the whole district.'

'A man of outstanding appearance. Perhaps living alone.'

Though that too was dead reckoning.

'Tomorrow . . .'

Bartram said: 'We can fix you up here, sir, if you'd sooner.'

But Gently shook his head, heaved himself up at last, set out to drive the roads once more.

At Heatherings, there was only the light in the hall, and a note by the telephone that said: *Wake me.* Gabrielle was sleeping with one arm outthrust. He moved it aside, didn't disturb her.

8

But then in the morning it was his turn: he awoke with the smell of fresh coffee in his nostrils. Gabrielle, smiling, fully-dressed, was just placing a cup on the cabinet beside him.

'What time is it?'

'Nine.'

'Oh . . . the devil!'

'Do not concern yourself, my friend. Upon the phone is this colleague, Mr Slatter, who instructs me to tell you there have been few developments. Also upon the phone, poor Andy.'

'Andy?'

'Are you not looking for large bearded men?'

'Oh lord – they haven't busted Andy!'

'Aha. But it is all sorted out.'

The painter, Andrew Reymerston, and his wife Ruth, had been in their company as late as the Saturday. A hefty six feet, he had that summer grown an impressive bird's-nest beard.

'What happened?'

'It is thus, my friend. Last night they have driven into Norwich for the ballet, and afterwards a little supper with friends. And so, they are returning in the small hours.'

'But he had Ruth with him!'

'He is putting the car away, Ruth has preceded him into the house. Then, up drive two gendarmes – "Monsieur, explain where it is you have come from!" Andy explains. They do not believe him. Ruth supports Andy. They do not believe Ruth. Then Andy hammers upon the table, says he is a friend of ours, also of Sir Tommy's. So they ring Sir Tommy, who is not greatly pleased to be hauled out of bed at such a time, and who, after confirming that Andy is a man of probity, tears several strips off these gendarmes. Thus, all is well, and the good Slatter wishes to convey his regret for this incident.'

Gently gulped coffee, hauled on a dressing-gown, went down to use the phone in the study.

'Sorry about what happened, sir –'

'Never mind that! Just bring me up to date.'

'Well, we've checked a few possibles, sir, but we haven't located chummie yet. There's a blacksmith over at Kirby who fits the description, but who claims he was tucked up with his wife. Then there's the basket-weaver at Rushton, but he only has an old blue van. Then Sheepbridge came up with a yachtsman, probably the one who was here on Sunday, only he took the morning tide, though they may catch up with him further down the coast.' Slatter paused. 'Then there was your friend, sir. But he did have a red car.'

'Just forget my friend!'

'Yes sir. I got a blast from the Chief Constable.'

'Nothing else?'

'One thing, sir. We've got the press boys here. And the television.'

'Stonewall them.'

'Also most of the village, sir.'

'I'll be there in under the hour.'

He hung up: the phone rang immediately.

'Gently . . . ?'

Sir Tom in person.

'Look, damned sorry about what happened to Andy, gave those two constables a piece of my mind. But how are things going? Are you on to that fellow yet?'

'We have descriptions from two witnesses.'

'I mean – know you're doing all you can! – but two on the trot. We need an arrest. Any prospect of that, is there?'

'We are combing the area.'

'Ha, yes. But I've had the confounded reporters ringing me. What do I say to them? I mean this damned fellow seems to come and go as he likes . . .'

Gently hung up again, swearing, and hastened to take his

shower. Yesterday Aspall had dealt with the single reporter who had found his way out to Harford.

'What's in *The East Anglian*?'

'You are headlined, my dear. Also, they have found up a very bad photograph. You will have breakfast?'

'No breakfast.'

But he grabbed a sandwich she had made for him on his way out.

If the square had been a popular venue yesterday, this morning it resembled a jamboree. Two television vans loomed over a jam of cars, and Bartram had posted a constable at the door of the police station. Women, children, men stood silently on the pavements, formed groups in any vacant space: they moved aside reluctantly to let the Rover thread through to the niche that Bartram had kept reserved for it. Flash-bulbs fizzed as Gently alighted.

'Sir . . . a statement!'

'Are you expecting an arrest?'

'If you would just say a word for the viewers . . .'

'Is it true that a local man is helping . . . ?'

Gently held up a hand. 'Later, boys!'

'Just a brief word for the early editions!'

'If you'd look this way . . .'

In the end he posed by the car and gave them what they wanted.

'We have an eye-witness description of a man we wish to talk to. He is above normal height and heavily bearded. He has been seen driving a red car. We wish to hear of any such man who has been seen in Harford or who is known to be resident in this area.'

'Does he have a name, Chiefy?'

'Is he a friend of Mrs Lound's . . . ?'

But that was all he was prepared to give them. And as he turned to enter the police station, there was a rush to the cars, to the vans. He was met by a harassed-looking Bartram.

'They've been at it, sir, from early on . . . and Mrs Burrows, she's been round here, wants us to issue a statement that her Markie is innocent . . .'

'Where is Burrows?'

'Lying low at home, sir. Somehow these press boys have got on to him. And according to her it's all round the village that he was picked up at the scene last night.'

'You have the scene covered?'

'Closed the road, sir. And I've got men patrolling the playing-field.'

In the office a no less harassed-looking Slatter was snarling at someone on the telephone:

'No, we don't need you to tell us – now hang up, you're blocking the line!'

'An anonymous call?'

'They're coming in fast, sir – crackpots in all shapes and sizes. But it's young Burrows they're gunning for mostly. With just the odd one tipping Gillings.'

'Anyone else?'

'Your friend Shavers to say it was ruining business last night. Seems people were staying at home, or just calling in there for a quick one.'

'No other prospects.'

'Not yet, sir. That blacksmith was the best one to date.'

Gently sat, filled his pipe. Suddenly, the police station was in a state of siege! The eyes of the village, the media, were raking it, expecting, demanding something to happen. And nothing was happening. Out there, the patrols were seeking, checking, questioning . . . here, nothing to check, no one to question: but here was where the world wanted to see some action! Now that the big man from the Yard had arrived, surely the drama was about to unroll?

The phone went: Slatter snatched it, listened: covered the mouthpiece with his hand.

'It's the lady.'

'Give her to me.'

Gently exhaled a stream of smoke.

'Mrs Lound?'

'Oh, you're back again, are you? I thought you must have sodded off somewhere . . .'

'You have a message for me?'

'Yes, I have. Can't you do something about my phone?'

'Your phone?'

'Yes, my phone. Every old bitch in the village is ringing me. And if it isn't them it's the newspaper blokes, wanting me to say I don't know what. Can't you do something?'

Gently said: 'We can monitor your incoming calls.'

'Monitor them . . . ?'

'Check the caller's identity before we allow the call to go through.'

'Oh.' She didn't sound enchanted. 'And is that all you can bloody well do?'

'You can leave the phone off.'

'Yes, that's nice, isn't it, and then I can't even hear from my friends.'

Gently said: 'Were you expecting a call?'

'Never you mind about that. Just you concentrate on Dracula.' She paused. 'I suppose you haven't got him yet?'

'We have his description.'

'His description?'

'Last night he was seen by witnesses.'

Another pause!

'You mean, you know just what he looks like?'

'We know that.'

'So what does he look like?'

'Like the man I described to you. But now we know he has a beard.'

'A beard!'

'A thick beard. Also, he drives a red car.'

'A red car . . .'

'Does that suggest someone?'

'I'm trying to think, aren't I? No, it doesn't.'

'The beard. The car.'

'All right, I heard! But it doesn't sound like anyone I know. Probably some poor bastard like Jacko. They all thought he was the one, didn't they?'

'Then you can't help me.'

'Get lost. And you can leave my phone alone.'

'You could just be at risk, Mrs Lound.'

'Pull the other one. All I see around here is cops.'

Hand on phone, Gently hesitated – worth ordering a monitor

anyway? But then the phone clattered again and he swept it up once more.

'Suffolk Constabulary.'

A breathy pause, then:

'Are you the bloke in charge of the murders?'

'If I could have your name . . .'

'But are you him?'

'You are speaking to the officer i/c.'

'Ah. Suppose.'

The local accent: the voice, that of a man of middle-age: in the background, a murmur of machinery: one was seeing the call-box by the quay.

'Listen . . . about Beattie. Haven't they told you?'

'Told us what?'

'About her brother-in-law.'

'Mrs Lound has a brother-in-law?'

'Course she have! Didn't you know?'

'Go on,' Gently said.

'W'him you're looking for, great big bloke with a mass of beard. Esau, that's who it is. Her old feller's younger brother. Esau. Esau Lound. Went away from here time she was married.'

Gently grabbed a pad. 'He went away?'

'Ah. They say he fancied Beattie himself. His brother set him up in the wholesale line, just before he buggered off to sea. And you didn't know?'

'Where is he now?'

'Why, up the river at Shinglebourne. Reckon he's the bloke you're looking for, that's time somebody told you.'

'And – your name?'

But the answer to that was a slow, deliberate hanging-up.

Gently shoved the pad to Slatter.

'Do we know about him?'

'No sir . . . we bloody don't!'

'The informant sounded sure of his facts.'

'Nor we didn't hear about him from Mrs Lound . . .'

About to dial, Gently hesitated again, then went for a different number. Answered the rolling voice of the Shinglebourne Inspector, Beamish.

'Gently here.'

'Good morning, sir! Wondered if we'd be hearing from you . . .'

'Listen. Do you have a resident by the name of Esau Lound?'

'Lound . . . would that be the fish-wholesaler?'

'Do you know the man personally?'

'Can't say I do, sir.'

'I want his description. Also the colour of his car.'

'If you'd hang on, sir . . .'

Echoey voices, sounds, somewhere the tatting of a typewriter; then:

'Sir, Detective-Constable Bidwell . . . I live almost next door to Mr Lound.'

'Describe him.'

'A very large man, sir, striking features, a heavy beard. A bit of a loner I'd call him, still has a boat and does some fishing.'

'And his car?'

'A red Lada Estate, sir.'

'Put the Inspector back on.'

Beamish was apologetic: 'Sorry, sir . . . just never struck anyone's mind . . .'

'I want to talk to Lound. Have him fetched in. I'll be with you in twenty minutes.'

'We'll have him here, sir, don't you worry . . . and I'm having a word with Bidwell . . .'

The break they were after? Action, at least! Outside, a fresh clicking of cameras: Gently, Slatter and Cox striding out to climb in the Rover.

'A fresh lead, sir . . . ?'

'Something for the stop-press . . . !'

But this time, not the whisper of a statement. Slatter got in with Gently, Cox in behind, and the Rover reversed smartly, making people jump back. Action stations! In his mirror, Gently could see the press men diving for their cars; then he was round the corner and away, boring down the narrow roads.

Deliberately he struck the back road and made good his escape from the bunch pursuing him. Doubtless they would ferret out his destination but, for the moment, a breathing-space. He kept the Rover boring, weathered Thwaite unobserved, swept solitary by marsh and heath into the small, seaside town of Shinglebourne. But, at the police station, Beamish met him with an anxious face.

'Sir, I'm afraid he may have skipped.'

'What?'

'He isn't at home, and his car has gone. Bidwell is trying to get a line on him.'

Gently smothered a curse.

'Where is his house?'

'Down at the town-end. The last before the causeway.'

'Jump in.'

Beamish got in with Cox, and they drove on down the Victorian high street. It brought them to the beginning of the long, shingle causeway, with the river to the right, the sea to the left. Old houses in a higgledy-piggledy terrace fingered out from the town, the last a storey higher than the rest, with a walled yard containing a timber-and-pantile structure.

'That's his cold-store . . . he buys off the fishermen, sells to the shops and hotels round about. Just a one-man business, but I daresay he does all right.'

'No trouble with him.'

'None. Bidwell says he drinks at The Fisherman's. Just sits in a corner with his glass, never a word to anyone except on business. And you think it was him . . .'

'He has questions to answer.'

'He's lived in the town nine or ten years now. Moved into this place six years ago, when he took up the wholesale business.'

'Has he always lived alone?'

'Bidwell thinks so.'

'Women?'

'None I've heard mentioned.'

Gently eased the Rover into the yard, of which the surface was sand with tufts of marram. The house was old, rambling, small-windowed, but kept well-painted and neat. The cold store was tarred: so too was the garage, standing empty with yawning doors. No attempt at a garden. From the cold store, the sudden murmur of a switched-on motor.

Bidwell came hurrying into the yard.

'We only missed him by a few minutes. According to a man

who lives up the road, his car went by about half an hour ago.'

'Towards the town?'

'Yes sir.'

This way lay the yacht club and Tom Friday's boatyard: the latter one could see, with two of the yard-hands, winching a yacht up his slipway.

'Of course he could be delivering fish, that'd be the usual thing with him . . .'

'You say he still keeps a fishing boat?'

'Yes sir. He nets a few drains up towards Thwaite.'

'Where does he moor?'

'Don't know that, sir.'

'Go and inquire of Tom Friday.'

Bidwell departed again. Gently strolled to the house, peered through his hands into windows. Behind one, a tidy kitchen, behind another, a sparse parlour. On a wall of the latter he could just make out the same photograph of the brother as that at Mrs Lound's, and, on the opposite side of the chimney-breast, a matching photograph of the lady herself. The latter, in an antique frame, had a fresh sprig of fuchsia stuck in the fretwork below it.

Beside Gently, Slatter murmured:

'Do you reckon he's hooked it, sir?'

Gently nodded to the telephone wires above.

'The moment she heard we had witnesses.'

'She must have guessed who it was from the start, sir.'

Yes, from the start; if it were he. But what strange bond was it that existed between the licentious woman and this solitary man? For six years . . . and now? One thing was plain: she was ready to protect him, if she might. Her body was another's for the asking, but her loyalty? That was something else.

Bidwell returned.

'He says up-river, sir. There's a bit of hard-standing by one of the drains. You can get a car out there down a loke.'

And the tide was going up.

'You stay here.'

With the others, he climbed back into the car. Beamish they dropped at the police station to issue an alert. The loke was soon found: a stony lane that shortly became a peaty marsh-track;

it wound between stands of fawny reed and flaking yellow bush-willow. Then:

'There's the car!'

A red Lada Estate was parked on a patch of brick-rubble. Beyond it, a drain wandered on through the reed-beds. And there were mooring posts. But no boat.

There was room to turn. Gently turned the Rover, parked, got out to feel the Lada's bonnet. It was warm. Once again, they could have been only minutes behind. A newish car, a 1500, in the back scoured fish-boxes and a wicker skep. Was it just possible that they were hunting, not a fugitive, but an innocent man going about his business?

'Sir . . . listen.'

From somewhere out on the waters was coming the faint throb of a boat's engine. Tantalisingly, one couldn't distinguish whether it was approaching or departing, passing up or down river: just the murmurous throb from beyond the reed beds.

'There's a bit of a path, sir . . .'

Along a margin of the drain, the ghost of a track.

'Cox, you wait.'

With Slatter behind him, he plunged into the slithery track, brushing past reeds, sere willowherb, leaning stems of giant nettles. It was further than one would have guessed. The drain wound on for at least two hundred yards, with the footing growing ever softer, the vegetation more obstructive. They came to huge posts equipped with some sort of tackle – a net, which Lound would have dropped to pass through; then, at last, to open water, the track ending at a marker post. And – too late! A blue-painted fishing-boat was chugging away from them up-river, at the helm a massive figure, a great back turned towards them.

'Lound!'

Gently bawled through cupped hands: the man at the helm must surely have heard him. But the head didn't turn, and the boat chugged on, making for the cover of the next promontory of reeds.

'Lound – come back here!'

He didn't want to know, kept on steering the boat ahead.

Seconds later he had reached the promontory, and the throb of the engine faded behind it.

'The bastard. What do we do now, sir?'

'Get back to the radio in my car!'

If the track had seemed long and obstructive before, it appeared doubly so now. Finally, panting, wet of foot, they regained the cars parked on the brick rubble; Gently crammed himself into the Rover and snatched up his handset.

'Get me Shinglebourne.'

Beamish came on.

'Sir, Lound has been reported heading for his moorings –'

'I know about that! Now he's away in his boat, going up-river.'

'Oh lor' – then you missed him!'

'I want the landings covered in that direction. Can you commandeer a boat?'

'Yes, Tom Friday –'

'Two men in a boat to follow him up.'

'You reckon he's running, sir . . . ?'

'I think it likely. And probably knows where he's running to.'

Beside him, Slatter whistled. 'To the lady, sir!'

Was there anywhere else for him to run?

Gently got his breath back, called up Bartram and put the Harford man in the picture.

'You think he'll come this way, sir?'

'It's on the cards. That he'll make for the landing where Burrows touched yesterday. Then work his way across country and try to contact Mrs Lound.'

'If he does we'll have him, sir. I'll put a car there.'

'Just remember you're dealing with a heavyweight. I've seen him. Three men if you can spare them, and warn them to be prepared for trouble.'

'Three men it is, sir.' Bartram hesitated, then: 'But if he doesn't come this way, sir? I mean, there are plenty of drains up that old river where a man could hide out.'

'In that case we may need a chopper.'

'Yes sir. Though he's a bloke who'd know where he was at.'

A bloke who would know . . .

What Lound knew now was that the police were on his trail, had almost caught up with him, were surely spreading a net that must take him if he stayed on the river. To get off it fast, wouldn't that be his aim, to put distance between himself and the neighbourhood . . . even if, for the moment, it meant postponing a possible refuge with the lady? To get off fast: to get away. And a man who knew where he was at . . .

Gently started his engine.

'Where to now, sir?'

'A place where this car won't be so visible.'

Slatter stared. 'But sir . . . you aren't thinking . . . ?'

'His transport is here and he just might try for it.'

He drove back to the road, turned, then eased the Rover down the loke again. He parked in the middle of the track just short of the final bend. The loke was narrow: the loke was blocked. Ahead, they looked over a hedge to the reeds and bush willows. And ahead, just out of sight, sat the red Lada Estate, unguarded, alone. Gently dropped his window. The only sound one could hear was a faint whisper from the reeds.

'He'd be a nutter to come back this way, sir.'

Gently shrugged: perhaps Lound was a nutter.

'If he went the other way . . . and then, after dark . . .'

But darkness was still six or seven hours off.

The radio spoke: Beamish again.

'Friday has fixed us up with a boat, sir . . . and I've put in cars up to Thwaite Bridge. Harford say they've got the other bank covered.'

'Any sightings reported?'

'No sir. I daresay he's holding close in to the reeds.'

'Let me know at once if he's spotted.'

'It may take a while to flush him out, sir.'

A whole scene going! But here, the peace of mid-morning: with even the reeds falling silent. Slatter stirred pensively, but held his peace; behind, Cox was lighting a surreptitious cigarette. And time was ticking by. If he meant to make a bold move, wouldn't Lound have chanced his arm by now?

'Boat on its way, sir.'

The voice on the radio was followed almost at once by the sound of an engine: the busy, high note of a powerful outboard, and the direction of this one never in doubt. From down-river its moan approached rapidly, passed by the drain, at once began fading: no sighting there. Then, without check, it melted away towards Thwaite. What had happened? Had Lound broken across-river . . . or, on the other hand . . . Gently reached for the handset.

'Any sightings?'

'Nothing yet, sir.'

'Is the boat in touch?'

'Just called in. They've rounded the point, can see the next landing, report no sightings up to there.'

Ten to one they had overshot him.

'Tell the boat to come back down.'

'Sir . . . ?'

'He'll have holed up in a drain. Fetch them back to begin checking.'

Was it to be a chopper job after all? The drains presented a formidable network: a network that Lound would have known from his youth, knew perhaps as well as any man going. Secret waters, on a rising tide . . . how long would it take to winkle him out?

But then:

'Sir . . . did you hear that?'

Cox, too, had dropped his window.

'A click, sir. I could have sworn . . .'

And then . . . no question! – the clap of a car door.

'He must have come through the marsh . . .'

'Get ready to take him.'

Silently, they dropped out of the car: Gently and Cox on one side, Slatter on the other. They had scarcely done so when a raucous engine clattered, and moments later the Lada appeared round the bend. It hesitated, jerked forward again, then came to an abrupt halt. The driver sat tight. A strange face was staring at them. Gently went round to the driver's door.

'Esau Lound?'

The man said nothing. Just the large eyes, staring.

A long face with a big, hooked nose and a trap-like mouth.

But no beard.

9

'What is the situation back there?'

'Just now it's pretty quiet, sir. The press boys don't know what to make of it. They tailed the cars that went to cover the river, and I hear they're still staked out there. Do you want the cars to stay, sir?'

'For the moment, yes. What about sightseers?'

'Same thing there, sir. Most of them have drifted off to feed the kids or get the old man's dinner.'

Lound himself hadn't spoken a word; nor had he given them a moment's trouble. At Gently's direction he had climbed out of the Lada and transferred to the back of the Rover: they'd had to push the front seat right forward for him, so that Slatter was riding in a knees-up posture. When the cars had been manoeuvred and they were driving away, the staring eyes had turned back to the Lada, just briefly; and Gently had rapped:

'Never mind the car! We'll take care of it.'

Then he had stared forward, over Slatter's head, glancing neither to right nor to left.

The same at the police station at Shinglebourne. He had marched from the car like an automaton, marched to the interview room, taken a seat on a chair that creaked under his unusual weight. And stared at nothing. Certainly not at the apprehensive constable who they'd put in with him.

'My goodness, those hands, sir!' Beamish had exclaimed.

Yes, the hands. And the ring on the finger. A signet ring larger than any Gently had ever seen, engraved with flowing, indistinguishable initials.

For the rest he was dressed in a clean tan slop pulled over a thick jersey, trousers that were almost pantaloons and wellingtons with rolled tops.

Six foot two? Three? Almost, it wasn't his height that counted. Rather the great shoulders, the barrel chest, the ape-like arms, clumsy legs. And of course the hands. And the piebald face, part ruddy, part grey: where the beard once had been. But now was not. And the staring eyes: tousled hair.

At forty or so, Esau Lound.

'We'll need a search-warrant.'

'No problem, sir.'

With Slatter he'd gone over that neat, rather bleak house, the house of a loner, one who saw no friends; and yet a house that held surprises. Lound was a reader. One end of the parlour had been shelved out for books. Books of travel, adventure, war; but also some literature, even philosophy. Then, a music-centre, with a few records that were quite unexpected. And on the walls a picture or two, beyond the taste of his sister-in-law.

Only these weren't what they had come to find: it was Slatter, frisking the bedroom, who struck lucky first.

'Sir – in here!'

Beside the dressing-table, a bin; and in the bin, wads of hair.

'She rang him, sir – and then he got rid of it.'

'Only, would there have been time for that? Between her learning that he had been seen and his departure from the house, not many minutes could have elapsed.'

'Wouldn't have taken long, sir, hacking it off with these.'

Handy on the dressing-table were a pair of nail-scissors. But Lound must have tidied his face afterwards with the electric trimmer which also lay there, still plugged in. Well, a mystery to be resolved.

'We want evidence to connect him with Beattie Lound.'

And for a long time it seemed there was none to find in the chilly, innocent premises. Clothes, out-size shoes, a well-stocked larder, tidy kitchen, an account book in a room used as an office, one suggesting that Lound wasn't short of a penny. Nothing to find? Back in the parlour, Gently gazed at the picture with its sprig of fuchsia . . . not evidence. But then he noticed it: the picture was standing proud from the wall.

'Here.'

Taped behind it, letters: letters in a sprawling, uneducated hand. Letters signed Beattie. Not so very many, but covering the whole period of the last six years . . .

'These will do him, sir. Do him right up.'

The letters brought the long, sad chapter to life, naïvely gave away a picture of a man entrapped in a hopeless infatuation. From the beginning:

'. . . I know he's gone, love, but you've got to understand. I had a rotten time, you know? Now I'm just going to live a bit . . .'

Then later:

'. . . No I'm not ready yet!!! And I don't care what you say. It's my life, isn't it, I've got to live it, and if you want to know I'm having a damn good time . . .'

Then:

'. . . you can stuff it, old bloke. I don't care what the bastards say. And never mind about God intending it, he'll have to wait a few years yet is what I say . . .'

And finally a letter a fortnight since:

'. . . Do you think I don't know what he's after? All the same he's a bit of a dear, could be worse, and his wife has hooked it . . .'

'The jury are going to love these, sir!'

Evidence in plenty: hard evidence.

'You can see that Barnby was the final straw.'

While Jackson just had a bit of bad luck.

'Fetch an envelope for these from the office.'

So far, so good: but it didn't end there. Now, on the phone to Bartram, something rather tricky to be arranged!

'We shall need an identity parade.'

He thought he could hear Bartram catch his breath.

'Can't quite see how we can manage that, sir – not with a chummie the size of this one.'

'What about those other fellows – the blacksmith, the basket-weaver, the yachtsman?'

'Well, we can try, sir. Don't know about the yachtsman, the last I heard he was still on the briny.'

'See what you can do.'

'Yes sir . . . we may have to make up with some of our own.'

In the interview room Lound sat unmoved, barely lifting his gaze when Gently entered. As yet they hadn't heard his voice, seen the trap-like mouth part. Didn't he care? Impossible to guess what was going on in that shaggy head. A loner, a man apart. And the fool of a selfish, worthless woman.

And at that it wasn't going to be so easy to smuggle Lound into the police station at Harford.

Forewarned by Bartram, Gently avoided the back road and chose the most roundabout of narrow ways, passing by chance a byre of lowing cows and an ill-kempt caravan, which had to be Gillings'. But, in the end, he must join the common road that led to the village and the square: and in the square he spotted him at once – the sentinel left there by the press men. He swung round hard into the parking.

'Wait a couple of moments – then get him inside!'

He jumped out, strode across to the reporter, who for a moment looked apprehensive.

'What paper are you from?'

'I'm *The Gazette*, Chiefy –'

'Right – just take this down. Today the hunt for the man the police want to question switched to the marshes around Thwaite . . .'

Nothing the reporter didn't know or couldn't guess, and maybe it wasn't fooling him either: but he was scribbling away at his pad while they were hurrying Lound through the back door.

'Do we get a name, Chiefy?'

'Later. Perhaps in time for the late editions.'

The man hesitated, but in the end went off to phone in.

A harassed Bartram was waiting inside.

'I've been on to HQ to send us some big lads. But beards, sir, where do we get them – that is, if beards still come into it . . .'

'And the others?'

'I've lined the blacksmith up, but I can't get in touch with the other two.'

'Send out for some food. And that goes for the prisoner.'

Lunch was baps and coffee in the office. Meanwhile a minibus arrived outside and decanted six stalwart officers in plain clothes.

Followed the smith, a handsome fellow but with a half-beard trimmed to a point; then the two witnesses, Gillings loudly complaining, Burrows trailing his mamma who, however, was denied entrance. Not very much room in that modest police station! The two witnesses were segregated in Bartram's office. Then the six officers and the smith were lined up in reception and Lound fetched from the one cell.

'You may take any position you choose.'

He simply added himself to the end of the line: not that it mattered. He stood out like a lamppost, with only the smith coming anywhere near him.

'Fetch Gillings.'

Gillings was instructed. Accompanied by Bartram, he moved down the line. He gazed with simple interest at each of the standees, and with particular interest at Lound. But:

'It's no bloody good, is it? The bugger I saw had a beard . . .'

'We think the man may since have shaved it off.'

'So there you are, then. How do I know him?'

'You caught a look at his face?'

'Ah. It was all beard. Now if it had been one of my milkers . . .'

In contrast to Gillings, Burrows seemed scarcely able to bring himself to look at the line-up. He moved by them, darting furtive glances, and barely that at the last one or two. Yet it was he who went back down the line and laid a tremulous hand on Lound's arm.

'It's him . . . I think.'

'But you're not certain?'

'Well, he's shaved his beard off . . . you can see . . .'

'Is that the only reason?'

'No! It's the shape of his head. Last night, seeing him against the light . . .'

'You may change your mind.'

'It's him. He's the only one as big as the man I saw.'

And that he stuck to.

The parade was dismissed, Burrows returned to his clamorous parent. Outside the hawks were gathering again: Gently lowered the blind of the office window. Slatter said:

'Do you think he'll talk, sir?'

Who could tell with that unusual man?

'He'd have piped up, you'd have thought, if he had a tale. He must know that we've got him bang to rights.'

Gently shrugged, took his seat at the desk, laid his pipe out before him. Something – what was it? – was making him uneasy about the silent man in the cell. Not his silence: it was his gentleness, his utter submission to his fate. From the first moment, out there on the marsh, he had offered not the smallest resistance. Simply, almost majestically, he had yielded. Why?

'Fetch him in.'

'Yes sir.'

Slatter went to the door and signalled.

'You don't have to say anything, but what you do say may be taken down and given in evidence. I would like from you a statement of your movements over the past forty-eight hours.'

He was listening to the preamble with his staring eyes just missing Gently: eyes that one saw were bluish grey, the colour of an unsunned sea. The chair he sat on was barely large enough, so that he was sitting with knees akimbo, the huge hands lying upon them, the monogrammed ring displayed.

On Gently's left sat WPC Joyce, pad and pencils before her. On his right, Slatter. At the door, a uniform man, with one of Gillings' trade-marks on his jaw.

Because the blinds were down the light had been switched on, which seemed to accentuate the odd variegation of Lound's features.

'For example . . . Sunday evening?'

'I wish for a Bible.'

And those were the first words they heard him speak. A deep voice, with the local inflection, but with an unusual and careful articulation.

'Why do you wish for one?'

'I will swear upon it.'

'We are not placing you upon your oath.'

'Nonetheless, I wish it.'

'This is not a court, Lound. Here, you are simply helping our investigation.'

'I will stake my soul upon my words. I would be believed. I shall swear that I am innocent of the crimes that you investigate.'

'You swear your innocence?'

'I did not kill these men. By the Father, Son and Holy Ghost. And this I shall repeat with the book in my hand, to whatever tribunal I must answer.'

'I'm afraid that won't do.'

'Then I am condemned who am innocent.'

'So, we shall take note of what you say. However, in the meantime we require a statement of your movements.'

'They are known to God.'

'But not to us. And until they are, you will be detained here.'

Silence, except for the scuffle of the WPC's pencil. No motion, no change of expression in Lound. In effect, he had no expression: one felt the man was buried somewhere deep behind those savage features. The pencil stilled.

'Do you wish to tell us?'

'I speak as one compelled by men.'

'Well?'

'On Sunday evening, the tide was running, I made an inspection of my nets.'

'At what time was this?'

'Some while after seven I drove to the mooring you have seen. I was about my business for several hours. When I returned to my house it was nearing eleven.'

'You have witness to that?'

'God's.'

'No witness.'

'I live alone. Also, I pursue my craft alone. None can say where I was or was not.'

'You realise what this means, do you? That you may well have been visiting your sister-in-law's?'

'God knows I was not.'

'But how shall we know it?'

'With the book in my hand, I will say the same.'

Gently said: 'With all respect to your beliefs, they are sometimes the resource of unprincipled men. What the law requires is something less doubtful. Can you prove where you were that night?'

Silence again!

'You could have been here in Harford. We believe you had

reason to visit Mrs Lound. She was under pressure from a man to accept his proposal. That man was Luke Barnby. And that man is dead.'

'God knows I didn't kill him –'

'But we don't know that! He was killed by a man of great physical strength. Also a man who wore a ring on his finger, a ring that left a distinctive injury.'

'You could . . . tell that?'

'Such a ring as you are wearing.'

'Many fishermen here wear such a ring.'

'But none of your physical capability. And with the motive that we know you to have.'

'I admit to no motive to kill.'

From a drawer of the desk Gently took the packet of letters they had found. He shook them free from the envelope, spread them out on the desk.

'No motive?'

Lound let his gaze fall on them. Impossible to tell if he were shaken. None of the usual signs of stress seemed to appear in this giant man.

'My brother's wife is an unhappy woman.'

'Killing two of her men-friends hasn't made her the happier. These letters make your infatuation with her plain. For years, you have been seeking to marry her yourself.'

'My brother would have wished it.'

'Never mind about him. Since his death you have been making overtures to his widow, perhaps hoping that in the end she would change her ways and fall into your hands. She and the money.'

'I care nothing for the money –'

'Listen. It was never her intention to marry Barnby. But she gives a different impression in her last letter, and that was the one that brought you to Harford. Barnby was a threat, a threat to be disposed of. It may be you intended merely to scare him off. But seek him you did, and when it came to the moment, your control snapped and you killed him. Wasn't that how it happened?'

'It was not I.'

'Who else with a motive so strong?'

'Others wear these rings.'

'Forget the ring! Do you deny that your object is to marry Mrs Lound?'

'I wish to bring her back. Back to love. Beatrice at heart is a loving woman. These things that she does are a penance, because in her heart she could not love my brother.'

'Because she loved you?'

'We are two souls. Souls God designed to come together. In her heart she knows this, she is not the woman of her deeds.'

'You regard yourself as her salvation?'

'There can be no other but I.'

Gently gazed at him – was it a con? If so, the execution was quite immaculate. Not by a flicker in the sea-grey eyes did the huge man give himself away. One had to believe it: as a sacred duty Lound was viewing his crass infatuation. And would that have made him less of a danger when his hands reached out towards a victim?

'On Sunday night, you were in Harford.'

'As He is my witness, I was not.'

'Very well, then. Where were you last night?'

The big man said:

'Delivering fish.'

That, at least, was provable: and a phone call by Slatter proved it. On the previous evening, Esau Lound had delivered fish to The Castle public house at Bradfield. The Castle had a restaurant, and the order was a regular one: on every Monday, Lound delivered fish. Then it was his habit to eat in the restaurant and to spend the remainder of the evening in the bar. He had been doing it for several years: he was known to the landlord and the regulars: beyond even unreasonable doubt, Lound had spent the evening at The Castle in Bradfield. Until closing.

'When did you leave Bradfield?'

At ten-thirty or a little after.

'How far is Bradfield from Harford?'

Apparently, a matter of five or six miles.

The map was produced again. Bradfield was a village in the vicinity of Sheepbridge: in effect, in driving between Bradfield and Shinglebourne, one passed within a couple of miles of

Harford. At any time after 11.00 p.m., on his own showing, Lound could have been parked where Burrows had placed the car.

'Did you make any phone calls while you were at The Castle?'

Lound paused, then said: 'One call.'

'To your sister-in-law?'

A longer pause.

'I wished to know if Beatrice was secure.'

'Secure . . . ?'

'She lives alone.'

'But – secure?'

'There had been evil done.'

'In fact, were you not enquiring if there was a police presence, prior to making a call upon her?'

'She is my only relative.'

'Just so. Yet we don't find you rushing to her side. All day yesterday you stayed away, though you must have heard what had happened here?'

A much longer pause!

'Beatrice rang me.'

'And, of course, advised you to stay away?'

'She thought it best.'

'Did she say why?'

When he didn't want to answer, his silence was quelling.

'She thought it best because your description exactly matches that of the man we were seeking. She denied that she knew such a man, though you must immediately have come to mind. Why should she do that?'

Silence!

'Wouldn't it be because she has suspicions too – roused at once by what happened to Barnby and, after last night, a moral certainty?'

And finally he was goaded.

'I have given her my word. Upon the book I swore it to her.'

'Very likely. But with her knowledge of you, how probable is it she would accept that?'

'In her heart, she knows me a true man.'

'She knows you as a man infatuated with her. A man who lives the life of a monk in the dream that one day she will relent.

A man who overlooks her every fault. Who she thought it was safe to tease.' Gently picked up a letter. 'And then her lovers begin dying, and in a way that could point in only one direction.'

'She has accepted my word!'

'What else would she dare do?'

'Beatrice knows I could never harm her.'

Gently shook his head. 'That went by the board when Luke Barnby was found hanging over her gate. She fears it now. She will always fear it. Any chance you may have had with your sister-in-law has gone.'

'I have spoken with her –'

'She fears you.'

'This is profanity you speak!'

At last a reaction in the grey eyes, a sudden jerk of the huge hands.

'We are two souls, souls intended. I am the protector of that woman.'

'Her protector against what?'

'Against evil. Against the sinning of the flesh.'

'Barnby? Jackson?'

'Against – evil. There is a dark power abroad. A dark power haunts her. Her weakness has raised it. It possesses a man who has lost his soul.'

'In short, a killer.'

'I pray for that woman. And I pray for that man.'

'For yourself.'

'For that man.'

'Who a witness identifies as you.'

'Then let that be as God wills it.'

The huge hands rose and fell. Then the staring eyes lowered, and once more Lound sat very still.

Gently said: 'This morning she rang you. No question of you being a protector then. We had your description, she warned you of that, and at once you sought to alter it.'

'As a free man I could watch over her.'

'Your actions were not those of an innocent man.'

'It were best I was free. The description I had heard. For my actions Beatrice is in no way responsible.'

'You heard it where?'

'It signifies nothing. On the radio I heard it. As a bearded man I was vulnerable. My deeds upon my head alone.'

'You intended to elude arrest.'

'For the sake of another.'

'For your sake alone you intended it. Mrs Lound you could only compromise, and perhaps terrorise in her own house. Was that the idea?'

'God forgive you for thinking so.'

'I think you killed two men, Lound. I think you are capable of killing again. I think only remaining in custody will stop you.'

'Then God's will be it.'

'You are admitting your crimes?'

'His will be done. But I am innocent.'

'Against all the circumstances? The evidence?'

'I am innocent. An innocent man.'

'But not in our eyes.'

He raised his staring gaze: there was torment in the massive face. Something he wanted to say, something that wouldn't clothe itself in words.

'Yes, Lound?'

'His . . . His will is strange.'

'Is that all?'

'You must – protect her.'

'She is not in danger.'

'Please protect her.'

Then the eyes sank again.

'Take him out.'

Slatter said: 'But didn't we ought to charge him, sir?'

Gently grunted. 'Time enough for that!'

Slatter looked askance. 'I don't know, sir. I'd say we had all we wanted there. You don't go for that Bible-thumping stuff?'

'First, I want a word with the lady.'

'Don't see we can get much more out of her, sir.'

'Beattie Lound has been protecting him.'

Gently lit his pipe: puffed meanly. Perhaps what he was wanting most was the rest of the picture! Depths there clearly were to that strange man which he was irritably aware that he hadn't sounded. Critical depths? He couldn't be certain: just that the need to know was urgent. And with a character as eccentric as that of Lound's, one didn't rush in to jump the fences . . .

'I thought it rather sweet, sir,' the WPC said. 'The way he feels about that woman. You can call it infatuation if you like, but I thought it was quite touching.'

Slatter said: 'He's a nutter, sir – religion and women, it's a bad mix. But we've got him nailed all right. The letters and all, he's for the high jump.'

'Still, you can't help feeling sorry for him, sir.'

That was the trouble: you were feeling sorry for him. As though he were some great animal, trained up to a creed that you couldn't quite grasp. A great bear, shambling, lonely, in a world inhabited by people . . .

'Get those notes typed up.'

'Yes sir.'

Gently lifted the phone and dialled.

'Mrs Lound . . . ?'

'Just you listen! I'm still being got at by those reporters. They say there's a manhunt on, and they think I can tell them who it is.'

'And have you told them?'

'Stuff it, will you? How do I know what sod you're after. Only they say it's a bloke in a boat, and that you've got men staked out at Thwaite.'

'Does that suggest someone?'

'Oh, lay off! Are you after a bloke, or aren't you?'

'We have arrested a man.'

'A man . . . ?'

'He is assisting us at the police station.'

A pause, equalling any of Lound's!

'Are you trying to tell me something, you bastard?'

'I would like to talk with you.'

'Yes, I'll bet. So you can just come round here, can't you?'

'Thank you, Mrs Lound.'

'You rotten so-and-so. Don't think you're getting any help from me.'

He hung up, went through to reception, and at once was button-holed by Bartram.

'The press have been crazing us for a statement, sir . . . somehow, they've guessed we've got chummie in here.'

'Tell them later. And recall those men.'

'Yes sir. Then there's this message from forensic.'

It mentioned the finger-ring again, adding:

'Of unusually large dimensions.'

10

Again the sun glowing through the trees on the knoll behind the house, the first miasmas of mist beginning to fade the drab marshes. No wind: on the far-flung moorings the distant yachts were painted motionless; all this coming into view as one crossed the rough playing-field.

Another such night arriving as the two which went before: but now the tiger had been caged, might not the night unfold in all innocence?

Gently had dropped the reporters at the near-side gate, which was still ribboned-off and guarded, but not before they had wrenched the statement they were sweating on from him.

'Have a heart, Chiefy, we'll miss the editions . . .'

'There's just time to get it on Five-o'clock News . . .'

In the end, at the gate, he'd turned at bay and set their eager pencils scuffling.

'A man answering the description of witnesses was arrested at noon today near Shinglebourne. He is being held at Harford Police Station and is assisting the police with their enquiries.'

'Has he been charged, Chiefy?'

'No charge has been made.'

'But you're expecting to charge him?'

'A charge may follow.'

'Have witnesses identified him?'

'A further statement will follow.'

And, quickly:

'Would his name be Esau Lound, Chiefy?'

'At the moment we are not releasing his name.'

'The sneaky sods!' Slatter exclaimed, as they passed through the tapes, while the reporters sprinted away. 'How do you think they got on to that, sir?'

'Probably the same way that we did.'

'You mean the anonymous caller?'

'He sounded like a fisherman. It probably earned him a few drinks. But they daren't print it.'

'All the same, sir. I'd like to give that bloke some quiet advice.'

Outside the house a car was stationed: they roused the occupant from a light doze.

'Anything to report?'

'Mrs Rivett has been out, sir. Went down to the shop to buy milk and papers.'

'Nothing else?'

'Just the lady at the window doing a Harvey Smith when she saw me.'

'Try to stay alert.'

'Yes sir. I'm due for relief in half an hour.'

A scene so peaceful: the bay-windowed house, the well-hedged garden, flaunting trees. Away down the road one could just see the bullocks looking over the gate to the marshes. But here that other gate, white-painted. And beside it the spot where two men had died.

'Come on.'

The wicket creaked as usual, and the sound brought a face to the window.

'You've got him, haven't you? You don't have to tell me! But what rotten sod gave him away?'

On entering the lounge, Gently had gone directly to the photograph which, after all, Mrs Lound hadn't destroyed. The same features, though not the same eyes. Here they were narrower, harder, more suspicious. Altogether they gave a wholly different aspect, the impression of a man as hard as teak. The elder brother. The man to whom Esau Lound had played a perpetual second fiddle.

'How much older was he . . . ?'

'What do you care. You've got your hands on Esau, haven't you? Norah was down there talking to the reporters. It's all over rotten Harford.'

'A couple of years?'

'Sod you. Count yourself lucky you weren't dealing with Aaron. He wouldn't have come in like a lamb, him. He'd have knocked your head off your shoulders.'

'Yet he it was you married.'

'Rub it in, go on.'

'You had your choice, and chose him.'

'So he was a bastard, a right bastard. But even then he was better than Esau.'

'And that remains your opinion?'

'Talked to him haven't you? Likely he'll get off from being weak in the head.'

'He was not your lover?'

'Give me some credit. If you want my opinion, the poor so-and-so couldn't do it.'

She was sober enough, but she was on edge, a drawn look about her snub-nosed face. It was the Rivett woman who had let them in, and now hovered, eager-eyed, by the lounge door. Mrs Lound had been seated, as usual, on the settee. She hadn't bothered to get to her feet.

'So now you're after me too, aren't you?'

Her tone also was more subdued – sulky, but half-resigned, some of the aggression gone out of it.

'You could have saved us a great deal of trouble. And Jackson probably his life.'

'I told you the truth. I never had such a bloke. And you never asked me about any relatives.'

'But you knew who the man was we were after.'

'Didn't know that either, did I. I mean Esau, who would have thought it? I'm not sure I'm going to believe it now.'

'That is hard to credit.'

'Please yourself. But I never thought he'd cut up like that. What you'd call a gentle giant, him – too gentle. That's his complaint.'

'Yet you warned him we were on his trail.'

'Warned him nothing. He wanted to come here.'

'Last night?'

'Yes, I'm telling you. I could hardly put the silly sod off. He was on the phone a couple of times yesterday, I was scared you were going to catch him at it. I mean all right, he was the sort you were looking for, but he was a relative and all that. I told him if he came anywhere near Harford he'd be running straight into your arms.'

'What reason did he give for wanting to come here?'

'I needed protection, he said. Going to protect me. Same thing when I gave him a ring this morning.'

'Following your conversation with me.'

'So all bloody right, what did you expect?'

'Tell me exactly what he said.'

'I've told you. He was coming out here to protect me.'

'To – protect you.'

Her hair swished.

'That fits in very nicely, doesn't it? First Lukey, then Jacko. And now you're saying he had his sights on little Markie?'

'We found letters you had written to him.'

'Oh charming. And of course you read them.'

'The last one refers to Barnby. It could have given the impression that you meant to accept him.'

'You rotten sod, reading my letters!'

'That was probably the impression Lound received.'

'You'll say that, won't you? And that set him off. He was going to save me from all these designing men.'

'Also the letters suggest that, however unlikely, Lound fostered hopes of winning you himself.'

'Oh gawd. And you're going to use them against him?'

'They will form one part of our case.'

She had jerked up straight, her eyes sparking.

'Now just you listen to me! It was all a game with Esau, him pretending that one day I was going to have him. I never saw him above twice a year – Norah here has never met him. Just we'd have a natter on the phone now and then, and he'd write me one of his silly letters. But serious? My foot. He's never had a woman, and wouldn't know what to do if he had one.'

'He was not at any time your lover?'

'No he wasn't. And another thing I'll tell you. I wouldn't know what to do either, not with a funny old lug like him. Aaron was different, he was a go-er, for all his holy joe capers. You want to know why I married Aaron? Because I thought the sod had got me up the spout.'

'Meanwhile, his brother was your ardent admirer.'

'I never said he wasn't, did I? We were sweethearts at school, me and Esau; Aaron never had time for the girls then. And that wasn't any big deal, either. Esau was scared of what Aaron would think of him. So we used to walk home, me one side of the road, Esau on the other, pretending he didn't see me. It was always like that. I said we were sweethearts, but he scarcely dared raise his eyes to me. Just that in the street, in the playground, somehow Esau was always there. In school, at my desk, if I looked up, sure enough I'd catch his eye. It got to be a joke. The other girls giggled at him, and Esau got pinker and clumsier than ever. Then he started leaving silly notes in my desk, and of course I pretended I'd never seen them. Oh, yes. It goes back a long way. But first and last it was just a game.'

'A game on your side . . .'

'On his too! That's the way some boys are, isn't it? And the men, he isn't the only one. Young Markie will grow up just like Esau.'

Gently said: 'Then you were no longer at school. You were a young lady helping at The Mariners.'

'So then it was a different sort of game, wasn't it, with plenty of blokes to give me the eye. And me so innocent, I could laugh. I let one bloke take me out in his car. A bit of a kiss and a cuddle, I thought, where my mum and dad couldn't see me. Well, I got out of that one, but it taught me what men were all about. For a long while after that I wouldn't let a bloke take me out in his car.'

'And Esau Lound?'

'I lost sight of him. I reckon the competition had got too fierce. And at first he was too young to come into the pub, though I believe he used to hang about outside. But it was Aaron I fancied the look of. He was a man's man was Aaron. Always a gang of blokes with him, though even then he was a strait-laced so-and-so. No swearing when Aaron was around, no loose talk about birds, that's what struck me about him. And sexy as hell. Though he didn't seem to know it. Well, an uncle or someone died and left them a cottage and boats at Wolmering, so that was the last I saw of them till their old man died, and they came back here. I remember them coming into the bar, Aaron and him, one Saturday evening, when the place was full of yachters and you could hardly hear yourself speak.

' "A pint for him. And one for me."

'And suddenly the devil was staring at me. Just like he'd never seen me before, never knew I'd existed.

' "Beattie, isn't it?"

' "Go on," I said.

' "You've come on a bit, haven't you?"

' "Come on yourself, Aaron."

' "You're a right woman now, you."

'And that was it. I could see he wanted me, and I was getting fed up with minding the bar. So like a bloody fool I led him on and said Yes the first time I was late. Well, you learn, don't you. But I always had an eye for big men.'

'And his brother stayed in the background?'

'From that first night. He was hovering around like Aaron's shadow. I was curious, I kept an eye on him, wondered if he would take up with a girl too. I mean by rights he should have pulled a bird, he looked as much of a man as his brother. But then I got it. He was still my sweetheart, though now he was having to lie low. He daren't catch my eye or pass a word, could scarcely bring himself to order a pint. So I teased the poor sod, you know? I couldn't help it. He acted so dumb.'

'How did he take it?'

'He just acted dumber, as though he didn't know what I meant. Then suddenly he backed off, didn't come into the pub any more. "What's happened to Esau?" I asked Aaron. He gave me a funny look. "Never you mind about Esau." And it's a fact that I never saw him again until he turned up at the wedding.'

'He came to the wedding?'

'He had to. He was Aaron's best man, wasn't he?'

'And then?'

'What do you mean, and then?'

'After you had become Mrs Lound.'

She pulled a face. 'He took off, that's what. We spent the honeymoon in Jersey. When we got back, no Esau. Aaron told me he'd gone to work a boat out of Shinglebourne.'

'Had the brothers had a row?'

'I don't think so. Just that Esau wanted to sling his hook.'

'Because of you?'

'What do you think?'

Gently didn't say what he thought.

'I'll tell you one thing.' She gave her head a toss. 'Bloody Aaron was jealous ever after. Not of Esau – I mean, who could be jealous of a shrinking violet like him? But he'd cottoned on that I'd been teasing Esau, and that was enough for a bastard like him. What a life. He wasn't above using the back of his hand, either.'

'You saw nothing of your brother-in-law during your married life?'

'Christmas, birthdays, times like that.'

'Social visits?'

'What are you getting at? Esau came here when Aaron asked him.'

'Phone calls. Letters.'

'He wasn't on the phone then, and it's a sure thing he wrote no letters.'

'But then all that changed, didn't it?'

'You sod,' Mrs Lound said. 'Now we're getting to it.'

The bar had clearly become irresistible, and she bobbed up from the settee. Gin gurgled from a half-empty bottle: she made no offer to anyone else. The Rivett woman looked as though she might welcome it; she was still standing by the door. Slatter had squatted on an arm of one of the big chairs, had been watching Mrs Lound with expressionless eyes. She poured and drank nervously, stared challengingly at her audience.

'You'd like me in the witness-box, wouldn't you? Well, you can forget that right away! If you're going to put that poor lug behind bars, it won't be with any help of mine. In the first place I don't believe he did it, he's just a great ox who's acted stupid. And in the second I'm telling you again, he knew he had nothing to expect from me.'

Gently said: 'Yet you wished to protect him.'

'Why not? He needs someone to look out for him.'

'A man who means nothing to you.'

'I didn't say that. Just I wouldn't marry him.'

'For him, you have taken quite a risk. You could be charged as an accessory after the fact. A man who means so little to you. Who you see only once or twice a year.'

'Oh, get lost.'

Gently said: 'I think you do have a fondness for that man.'

'I thought you said you'd read the letters.'

Gently stared at her. Then nodded.

'Sod,' Mrs Lound said.

She resumed her seat, smoothed her skirt, took a pull from the glass.

Gently said: 'Your husband won that money. I'm told he acted well by his brother.'

'So what. They were always close, those two. Perhaps I was the one who should have been jealous.'

'He set him up in business.'

'He bought out old Yaxley. That didn't cost him a bomb. And if you're thinking it was the money Esau was after, you can forget that for a start.'

'His brother's money.'

'I'm saying, forget it.'

'He could have used it to expand his business.'

'Are you serious? Enough to rub along on, that's all Esau ever wanted. If he'd had Aaron's money, like as not he'd have given it away. So forget it. He wasn't after it. It would have scared him more than I did.'

'The money came. The business was bought. Surely you'd have seen more of your brother-in-law then? There would have been expeditions to look it over, visits here to settle the finance.'

'That was all between them, wasn't it.'

'Then, when he moved in, a house-warming?'

'Can't I get you to understand? It was him and Aaron, me tagging along.'

'By then, you were perhaps less enchanted with your husband. You had found him to be a tyrant and a brute. So different from his gentle brother. Who had worshipped you in secret for most of his life.'

'You lousy bastard.'

'When Aaron was around you had to toe the line of course, but he couldn't be around the whole of the time, and, with respect, you were no novice at the game.'

'I'll sling this drink at you!'

'This time, you didn't make the mistake of being obvious. You knew your man. Esau was a romantic. Also, he would never countenance betraying his brother . . . or would he?'

Her eyes were hating him.

'At least, there was a little pleasant understanding! You would if you could and, perhaps, when time was . . . ? Secret looks, words, little actions of significant meaning. A delectable basking in a devotion the like of which you never got from your husband. And he feeling guilty, no doubt, but caught in a romantic daze . . . could this be sin? He understood readily that you were unhappy with his brother.'

'I could kill you!'

'And then the phone calls, notes passed, it may even have been clandestine meetings. Though you had to put up with Aaron, always this little sweetness in the background. A game, you called it, a pretty game. You knew the rules, and so did Esau. Nothing to hope for, nothing to complete. Because, always, Aaron was standing in the way.'

'Bastard!'

'And then, one day, he didn't.'

'It wasn't like that at all, you sod.'

'After which, we have your letters. We can easily trace the affair from there.'

'My letters . . . nothing!'

'Aaron had gone. His bold, harsh spirit had found its own fate. Just the photograph left on the wall, and a sense of relief that one can well understand. But the shield had gone too. You were suddenly vulnerable to the expectations of the brother, expectations which you had not the smallest wish to fulfill. You had suffered, you were going to live. Marriage you had found to be too onerous. You had the means, the physical attraction, and Esau would have to be put in his place.'

'I tell you it wasn't like that!'

'We have the letters.'

'Sod the letters. All right, I didn't want to marry him, and he just wouldn't take no for an answer. So what was I supposed to do?'

'In effect you carried on the same game. Only now, in place of Aaron, you had one lover after another.'

'And didn't that show him?'

Gently shook his head. 'Any ordinary man, yes. But not this one. Believe it or not, but I think Esau Lound understood you.'

'Understood me my foot!'

'Understood you. That there was more to you than mere promiscuity. That you were reacting to a loveless marriage, would one day transcend it, come out from the shadow.'

'And marry him?'

'And marry him.'

Now she was staring with large eyes.

'This is just what you want me to believe. The way you're going to put it in court. He bloody knew there was no chance, never had been from the beginning.'

'Esau Lound thought there was.'

'Not after all these years – no! After all the blokes . . . even Esau! He would have to be nuttier than I thought.'

'All that he was ready to forgive.'

'I've lost count.'

'One or a dozen. It didn't matter.'

'A dozen, don't make me laugh. And I don't want the sod to forgive me. He told you all this?'

Gently nodded.

'Then he's raving, that's what it is. Or you're twisting him up with your rotten questions, getting him to say whatever you want.'

'It could just be true.'

'Bloody stop it!'

'Waiting and watching. For six years. Certain his time was going to come. That what he saw as God's will would prevail.'

'Stop it – do you hear?'

'Isn't that how it was?'

'Oh lord. Let me have a drink.'

She tipped up what was left in the glass, rose shakily and went to the bar for more.

'You'll have me believing it next. I know that Lukey upset him. He was on the phone. All that holy joe stuff. And of course I had to bloody well tease him.'

An exclamation from Slatter!

'You teased him about Barnby?'

'Well, he was asking for it, wasn't he. It was after that letter. Told him I was getting soft, maybe the wedding-bells would tinkle after all. Said he could be my best man again, that I'd square it for him with Lukey.'

'What was his reply?'

'Quoting scripture, the lug. That stuff about God's will and all. Oh, he was all right. And in the end I told him that, maybe, I wouldn't go overboard this time.'

'When was this?'

'Sometime last week. The same day he'd have got the letter.'

'And that was your only contact with him?'

'Until he rang yesterday, wanting to come here to be my protector.' She drank tremblingly. 'But I can't believe none of this.'

'To be your protector. That was the message?'

'What he said.' She shuddered. 'Same again when I rang this morning.'

'Did he seem disturbed?'

'Suppose you could say that. Didn't sound like the same old lug at all. Going on that he was really worried for me, ought to be here on the spot. I told him not to be crazy, you'd arrest him for certain, it was him who needed protecting. But he kept on. Last night . . .' She drank quickly from a slopping glass.

'What about last night?'

'I don't know. He seemed so set on coming here. I lied, said there was a copper still out there. But I'm not certain if he believed me.'

'You didn't see him?'

'God, no. Just bloody Jackson at the door.'

'Burrows was also there.'

'I never saw him.'

'He identified Lound in a line-up.'

She'd been standing; now she sat again, glass clasped in both hands.

'I've got to believe this, haven't I?'

Gently nodded. 'I'm afraid you'll have to.'

'That Esau . . .'

She crouched over the glass.

For some reason, the Rivett woman was sniffing.

They left the house when the sun was gone and the flash of the beacon just beginning to show. To the man sitting in the car, Gently said:

'All right . . . you can report back in!'

Wasn't the tiger caged?

On the darkling square only a few reporters were now kicking their heels round their cars. But they were on the alert at once when they caught sight of Gently and Slatter.

'Look – Chiefy! All the world knows it's Esau Lound you've got in there. Tomorrow you'll be running him before a beak . . . couldn't we just have his name now?'

'Where did all the world get this information?'

'Oh, come on! We can't tell you that.'

'A straight swop.'

'We can't, Chiefy. Let's say there's this pub, not a hundred miles away.'

'He wasn't one of ours.'

'Now, Chiefy, would we –'

Gently shrugged. 'Go ahead and print.'

Moments later they were standing alone, their only audience a few hardy gapers.

'Do we charge him now, sir?'

'Let's talk to him.'

The one cell in the police station was small but sufficient: a toilet, a varnished wooden bunk, and space for three strides up and down. Lound sat on the bunk, his knees cocked, head between the huge hands. Visible the big ring, the swirling monogram engraved upon it.

'Lound.'

He didn't look up.

'We've been talking to your sister-in-law, Lound.'

Now he did.

'Last night, she tells us, you were very insistent when you made that phone call.'

The tormented grey eyes stared.

'You did come to Harford, Lound, didn't you?'

'I wished to be beside her.'

'You came. You parked your car down the road from the house.'

'No.'

'You were seen running towards it. When the body was still swinging over the gate.'

Just the shaggy head shaken.

'Then later – you remember? – when you were driving from the scene. Driving very fast. You were nearly in collision with a car that was turning in the road.'

'No.'

'You don't remember? But the other driver remembers very well. A large bearded man. In a red car. Driving very fast from the direction of the village.'

'A . . . bearded man?'

'A bearded man. Which is what you were last night.'

'And the car . . . ?'

'A red car.'

The grey eyes, staring, staring.

'Do you still deny this?'

'Last night she was alone.'

'Oh yes. The policeman she warned you of had departed.'

'Without protection.'

'She scarcely needed you! The man who died had only come there to speak to her.'

'A lover.'

'Yes, a lover. The conversation they had made that pretty plain. And you were there. You heard that conversation. Saw the man returning down the drive when the door was closed on him.'

'The poor fellow.'

'Is that all you can say?'

He'd buried his face in his hands again. Because the bunk was so low, his posture looked absurd, the knees cocked almost as high as the head.

'God's will be done. He must watch over her.'

'Lound, against whom did you think you were protecting her?'

'Against the power. Against the evil she has released.'

'The evil in you?'

'Leave me. To pray.'

Bartram, waiting with the key, touched his head.

'A fiver it never comes to court, sir! Your friend Shavers was on the phone . . .'

And Gently almost snarled:

'To hell with Shavers!'

11

To charge Lound and get it over? That was what everyone seemed to be expecting – Slatter, Bartram, the reporters' night-watchman, and now, on the phone, even Sir Tom.

'Had to congratulate you, George. Aspall rang me with the news. Quick action – that was what we needed, and quick action is what we've got. How did you get on to the fellow?'

'An anonymous tip-off.'

'Got him cold, have we?'

'He has no alibi, we have evidence of motive, and a witness has picked him out in a line-up.'

'Good enough to go ahead?'

'It's a very strong case.'

'Charged him, have you?'

'Probably tonight.'

'Don't waste any time, George. Know I mustn't interfere, but it would help the image if we beat the deadline with the press. Took a bruising last night, you know. Need to show the public we're on our toes.'

'I'm hoping for more co-operation from Lound.'

'Be nice, of course. But with a case that strong . . .'

Meanwhile, at Heatherings, Gabrielle was wistfully hopeful that the arrest meant his early return.

'Supper shall be cold, my friend. If I am soon to see you . . .'

But something made him reply:

'Don't expect me.'

Slatter said, doubtfully: 'Are you thinking he'll cough, sir?'

But no, it wasn't that either. So, what was it? Still that unease, the feeling that as yet there was ground uncovered. He didn't know all: Lound was still resisting him: he couldn't put himself inside that man. Was it simply the contrast between the crimes and seeming gentleness of the fellow – a sensation that, however powerfully motivated, such extremes of violence were outside his character? But Gently had known other Jekyll-and-Hyde killers, men as apparently inoffensive as Lound, who, nevertheless, and often with slight motive, had committed such insane acts. Did Lound have a doctor . . . ?

Almost without thinking, he found himself dialling Capel's number. Either Lound was on the Shinglebourne doctor's list, or Capel would know whose list he was on.

'Gently here.'

'You old ruffian. I've just heard the news on the radio. You've gone and pinched our Esau, of all the least-likelies in the place. Surely you can't be serious?'

'You know Lound?'

'Know him? Tanya buys our fish off him. That plaice you thought so highly of last weekend was supplied by the local Goliath.'

'Is he on your list?'

'He is. And as sound a specimen as you'll find.'

'It's his mental condition that interests me.'

'Oh . . . I see. Then this is serious.'

'I admit that he puzzles me.'

Capel hesitated. 'This would rate as privileged information, if I had any. Only I haven't. To the best of my knowledge, Esau is thoroughly *compos mentis*. A bit of an old eccentric, of course, but I wouldn't put it any higher. And don't let the simple fisherman angle fool you. Behind all that he's an intelligent man.'

'A religious fanatic.'

'Give him that. But it's not unusual among the fisherfolk. I imagine men pursuing that trade often feel uncomfortably close to the Almighty.'

'There's a very strong case against him.'

'Oh dear. Is he a schizo, you're going to ask.'

'That's what I'm asking.'

'And the plain answer is I don't know.'

'A man whose whole nature could suddenly change.'

'Yes, you don't have to rub it in. I suppose it's possible. Except that I'm his doctor, and never for one single second suspected it. You're reasonably certain – that he's your man?'

'On the facts I would have to say so.'

'Well, hear me say that it's a shock. And will be to a lot of people.'

'But – with such a man – possible?'

'You're screwing it out of me and I have to say it. Yes, it is. But what a blasted world we live in – and for once, old son, I hope you're wrong.'

Capel hung up on him; he hadn't wanted to make even such a modest concession. And it amounted to little, certainly not the authoritative word that Gently was seeking. But one phrase stuck: Esau Lound wasn't the 'simple fisherman' he appeared: no, he was intelligent. And in this context, might not 'intelligent' equate with 'devious'?

The phone rang: he swept it up.

'Chiefy –'

Gently snapped: 'What do you want, Shavers?'

'No need to jump down my throat, Chiefy! Is it right you've nabbed Beattie's brother-in-law?'

'What about him?'

'Look, I'm trying to help. You remember Ted Moulton? Well, I've got him here now, and he can tell you a few things about that geezer.'

'Things you've primed him with?'

'Now, Chiefy! He couldn't take a lot more booze anyway. Those press boys were lushing him up, it won't cost the special fund a penny.'

'The press boys, eh?'

'They were here earlier . . . honest, I tried to shut him up.'

Well, well.

To Slatter, Gently said: 'You hang on here.'

In reception. Bartram beckoned to him, mimed for him to hearken. From the cell, one could hear the muffled strains of Lound singing 'Eternal Father'.

One went down two steps into the bar of The Mariners, a low-ceilinged, flag-floored establishment with a great brick hearth at the far end. Shavers was waiting for him.

'There he is, Chiefy, and don't let him kid you he's Brahms and Liszt. I've seen him put away his dozen and then walk home afterwards.'

The large, moon-faced fisherman was seated next the hearth, gazing sadly at the lees in a glass. But a handful of others were in the bar, all fishermen, among them Burrows, who avoided Gently's eye.

'Do I top him up?'

'Just fetch me a pint.'

One went down another step to approach the hearth. Gently took a seat next to Moulton's, held out a hand towards the wood-fire. Shavers bustled up with the pint. Gently drank, looked Moulton over.

'You know me?'

'Ah. Knows you.'

'You've been shooting your mouth off, Moulton.'

'Don't know about that.'

'You've been talking to reporters. When you should have been talking to us.'

'Ah, well. They was gentlemen, wasn't they?'

'Meaning they filled you full of beer.'

'Yes, and that's more than the old coppers would've done.' He mopped the big face. 'Anyways, I let on to your lot first. Because some bugger had to tell you, didn't they? You weren't getting nowhere on your own.'

'But you didn't give your name. Like an honest man.'

'Told you what you wanted to know.'

'So now you're going to tell me some more.'

'Reckon. And reckon that's worth a wet.'

Gently considered him, then signalled to Shavers. Shavers collected Moulton's glass. Up the bar they had fallen silent, though no faces were turned towards the hearth. Behind the counter a shutter had flicked back, revealing Myrtle's curious face. Shavers returned. Moulton drank deep, wiped his mouth with the back of his hand.

'Sunday night, then.'

'What about it?'

'Esau. He was over here. See him. Never spoke to him. No bloody pal of mine, Esau.'

'You saw Lound in Harford?'

'Reckon. Dark, wasn't it, but I knew him. Him and his damn great beard. Swear it in the court, I will.'

'At what time was this?'

'After turn-out. I'd been down to my store, never you mind why. See him cutting across the square as I was on my way home.'

'Coming from which direction?'

'Why hers.'

'Heading which way?'

'Towards the Castle. Got his car parked there, I reckon. Down where no one wouldn't see.'

'You heard a car start?'

He wiped his mouth.

'I'd be home by then, reckon. But that was Esau cutting across the square, so there you are, old partner.'

'Though you say it was dark you could still be certain?'

'Could see enough for that, couldn't I?'

'How many pints had you put away?'

'Never you mind. That was Esau.'

He swallowed beer, set the glass down, flickered Gently a look from muzzy eyes. A clincher handed on a plate . . . ? Up the bar you might have heard a pin drop.

'You tell me that Lound is no friend of yours.'

'No friend of any bugger's, is he? Great big sod, I went to school with him, never could get on with Esau.'

'In fact you don't like him.'

'Ah, who does?'

'But don't you have a particular reason?'

Moulton stirred his large gumboots: up the bar someone tittered.

'Nothing to do with it, is it? See him there like I say. Beard and all, I could see that. Same like young Markie last night.'

'Same like young Markie?'

'Believed him didn't you? Leastways, that's what he's been telling us.'

Gently turned, fixed an eye on Burrows, raised a crooked finger. Awkwardly, the pale-haired young man rose, came reluctantly down the bar. Now Myrtle had had her head through the hatch, Shavers was lounging by the end of the counter.

'You have been talking too, Burrows?'

'Yes – but I didn't talk to the reporters!'

'Just to your mates.'

'I thought it was all right – I mean, now you've got him put away . . .'

'How, though it was dark, you saw this man well enough to pick him out in a line-up – even though he'd shaved his beard?'

Quite literally, Burrows bit his lip.

'Ah, and you believed him,' Moulton said.

Gently eyed him. Moulton wiped his mouth, swallowed another gill of beer. Gently said:

'What is your grudge against Lound?'

'Never said I had one, did I?'

'I'm waiting.'

Moulton stirred his boots. 'Did me out of the Black Drain, didn't the bugger. Me, who'd had nets there since his brother's time, should've had the Black Drain by rights.'

'He reclaimed a fishing right?'

Moulton drank beer.

'And now you're getting your own back.'

'Nothing to do with it.'

'First you put the squeak in. Now you're trying to push him under.'

'I'm telling you, I bloody saw him.'

'And I'm to believe that?'

'Isn't he the sort of sod who'd do a job like that?'

'Is he?' Gently said.

Moulton drank beer.

'I went to school with the bastard,' he said.

'Fill them up again.'

Moulton ran on beer, and now wasn't the time to let him go dry. Shavers hastened to collect the fisherman's glass and to set a fresh pint before him. Burrows took the opportunity to retreat up the bar, but took a seat at no great distance. Myrtle, meanwhile, had reached through the hatch to fix herself up with a short.

Moulton poured beer into himself. Gently drank. Moulton breathed gustily. Then pointed to his ear.

'See that?'

The ear was misshapen.

'What Esau did to me when we were kids. Because why? Because I stoned his dog when it had pissed over my bike.'

'He struck you?'

'Bloody near killed me. That lug has never been the same since. Then another time, when we'd set light to a hut he'd made out of reeds. Went off his nut, nearly busted my ribs. I was feeling it for days.'

'Didn't his brother intervene?'

'What? There's some can tell you about him, too. A couple of right bastards they was. But Aaron was older than us, wasn't he?'

'Esau was unpredictable.'

Moulton drank beer.

'Always sweet on Beattie, did she tell you? She showed us a love-letter what he'd writ, a big laugh we had over that. Chased us all over the marsh he did, would have killed some bugger if he'd caught them. Don't you worry. Right from a kid. You've got your hands on the right bloke.'

'He was quick to anger.'

'Couldn't trust him could you? His brother now, you knew where you were with him. No one cheeked Aaron, they knew better. But Esau would cut up all of a sudden.'

'And . . . when he grew older?'

Moulton wiped his mouth.

'Up there at the nets in the Black Drain. Warned me off them, he said. The bugger caught me. Threw me clear back into my boat. That was five years ago, but you don't forget a thing like that.'

'And you haven't forgotten.'

Moulton drank beer.

'In the dark, you saw Lound crossing the square.'

'I'm telling you.'

'Lound and no other.'

'The big bearded sod,' Moulton said. 'I saw him.'

'An hour or more after turn-out, and you just happened to be there.'

'I can't help it,' Moulton said. 'I saw him.'

'I shall need a written statement from you.'

'Oh, bugger that!'

And the muzzy eyes slid away from Gently's.

At the bar a telephone purred: Shavers took it. He beckoned to Gently.

'Some geezer who doesn't give his name . . . wants to talk to the cop in the bar.'

Gently picked up the receiver.

'Yes?'

For an instant, thick breathing. Then a muffled voice:

'You're holding Lound. He didn't do it. Let him go.'

'Who is this speaking?'

'One who knows.'

'I shall need your name –'

'Just the message.'

And the caller hung up: he had sounded almost in the next room.

Another crank? But the voice had had a nervous, urgent quality. Gently slammed down the phone.

'Which is the nearest phone box?'

'It'd be the one on the quay. But if you're wanting to make a call, Chiefy –'

Gently brushed Shavers aside, headed for the door: in passing, he noticed that Burrows was missing.

He saw the young fisherman again on the quay by the faint radiance from the phone box.

Which now was empty.

'Who was in that phone box?'

'Someone . . . I didn't see.'

Burrows had turned towards him in alarm. He was standing by bollards from which ropes descended into blackness, no doubt to a boat.

'I thought . . . I didn't know you wanted me . . .'

'Tell me exactly what you saw.'

'Well . . . nothing, really! Just someone making a call. His back was towards me, and I didn't stare . . .'

'A big fellow?'

'I didn't notice . . .'

'His clothes?'

Burrows simply goggled.

'I was just going past to look at my moorings . . . I heard the door shut, but I was feeling the lines . . .'

'Did you hear which way he went?'

'No! I was just bending down to ease the springs . . .'

Whoever he was, the caller had had no time to escape past The Mariners. That left the hauled-out boats in one direction and the shelving banks and the marshes in the other: a hopeless prospect. And either way, he could work back into the village. Unless . . .

'You left the company in a hurry, didn't you?'

'Me . . . ?'

'What was the rush to check your moorings?'

The caller had muffled his voice: tucked into Burrows' bomber-jacket was a scarf, probably knitted by his mother.

'I . . . I just wanted . . .'

'One moment you're all ears, the next you've quietly faded away. Then the phone rings, and somebody who knew I was in there asks for me. Did you make that call?'

'I . . . no!'

'I come out to find you a few yards from the box.'

'But there was someone in there!'

'So where did he go?'

'I . . . look, I never made any call!'

'Always one finds you on the spot, Burrows. And it was you who picked out Lound in the line-up.'

'But I was certain it was him . . .'

'While now you're not?'

Burrows was gazing with frightened eyes.

'Look, it was dark . . . like you said . . .'

'You wish to withdraw that identification?'

'No . . . I don't know. I was doing my best. But if it's going to rest on that, like . . . well, I didn't see him proper, and if you say there's someone else . . .'

'The caller just now said it wasn't Lound.'

'Nor it wasn't me who made that call!'

'And he said another thing.'

'I tell you it wasn't . . .'

'He implied that he knew who the killer was.'

'Oh dear!'

His gaze was darting about, as though once more he intended to run for it. But Gently was planted firmly before him, and only black water lay behind.

'Do you know who he was?'

'I don't. I don't!'

'Yet you of all others have been closest to him. On Sunday, and again last night. On your own showing, you have seen this man.'

'I saw old Gillings –'

'Not Gillings.'

'So then it's him. They're all saying it's him.'

'But what do you say?'

'I don't know! I've done my best, that's all.'

Gently said: 'This man is dangerous and wouldn't hesitate to kill again. If you know he isn't Lound then you'd better tell me. In case you go the way of the others.'

'Oh lord, but I don't know. Nor I didn't make any call.'

'This had better be the truth.'

'It is, I swear it.'

'So why did you come out here?'

'It's the bottom of the tide . . .'

And it probably was. A little down the quay protruded the mast of some low-lying craft, while the ropes looped to the bollards descended steeply into the darkness. Mist, dark and silence. If the caller were not Burrows, the night had long since swallowed him up.

'My advice to you is to go home.'

'I – I left my drink in the pub.'

Gently shrugged. Besides themselves on the quay, not a soul to be seen, a sound to be heard. Just the light from the phone box and, up the road, from the windows of the pub. Had the caller peered in at those windows, seen him sit there, interrogating Moulton?

'I – I think it was him. The man I picked out.'

Someone, at least, taking Lound's part! And a local: his prompt retreat suggested a familiarity with his surroundings. But the voice had been successfully muffled, one couldn't have sworn to a trace of accent.

'Now you've got him, wouldn't it be all right . . . ?'

Burrows' confidence was returning.

'I mean – only if she wanted it! I could give her a ring first . . .'

Gently gazed at the pale, anxious face.

'Haven't you learned your lesson yet, my lad? Beattie Lound is no woman for you. And just now she has other things on her mind.'

'Then you don't think . . . ?'

'Just stay away from her.'

Burrows looked genuinely dashed.

'I'm the only one left. So I thought . . .'

'Stay away. And that's an order.'

They marched together off the quay, up the street; re-entered The Mariners. Moulton hadn't stirred. Shavers was saying to the phone:

'. . . he's just walked in!'

Gently took the phone: Slatter.

'Another one of those comic calls, sir. Chummie saying as how Lound never done it and we'd better let him go.'

'A chummie talking through his scarf?'

'It's what it sounded like, sir.'

'How long ago?'

'A few minutes.'

Which ruled out Mrs Lound's most obstinate lover.

Meanwhile Shavers was eyeing Moulton:

'I hope you don't think I put him up to it, Chiefy . . . !'

And Burrows was nursing an almost empty glass, sitting hunched, sitting alone.

'Mrs Lound?'

'Not you again. Can't I even have a meal?'

In fact Gently himself was eating one more sandwich, sipping one more mug of instant coffee. He could have done better: on the counter at The Mariners had stood a blackboard chalked with fare. Instead, he had returned to the police station to share this bleak repast with Slatter.

Lound had sung more hymns, Bartram had told him, and had rejected an offer of sustenance. Now he was silent, but through the spy hole Gently could see him kneeling, apparently in prayer. An awesome figure! Even on his knees, his head reached well-nigh the height of a man. His eyes were closed, lips moving soundlessly, huge hands clasped at the level of his thighs.

'Put a tray in there.'

'He won't touch it, sir.'

Were they in for a hunger-strike, along with the rest?

In the office, he'd found Slatter brooding over the typed copy of Lound's interrogation. No need to guess what the local man's thoughts were: the eyes that greeted Gently were wistful. But they'd brightened up when Gently had told him of Moulton's claimed sighting.

'The right time and right place! He's never going to pray his way out of this, sir.'

'Only we can't use it.'

'Sir?'

'In my opinion the testimony is doubtful.'

'But . . . if this Moulton is ready to swear?'

'Take it from me. The D of P's office wouldn't accept it.'

'But we could put it in, sir . . .'

Gently grunted.

'What was your impression of the fellow who made those calls?'

And over the sandwiches, the coffee, still that voice on the phone was troubling him. So certain of itself it had sounded, as though asserting what could never be in doubt. The voice of one who knew . . . And in the end, he'd pulled over the phone.

'About your brother-in-law, Mrs Lound. Would you know the names of any of his associates?'

'Norah has just dished up some grub, and you're dragging me away for this?'

'If you would be so kind . . .'

'Doesn't have any, does he? If you don't know that you haven't found out much. Lives on his tod, always has done, that's the sort of bloke he is.'

'But a few people he must know . . . ?'

'You tell me. Except maybe the ones he does business with.'

'Perhaps one close friend?'

'Then it's a dead secret.' She paused. 'Just what are you on about now?'

Gently said: 'A call from a man. A man who would appear to be a friend. Who doesn't want his voice to be identified. Wouldn't you know of such a man?'

'What's he saying?'

'That doesn't matter. But if we can find him it may benefit Lound.'

'You mean . . . ?'

'Do you know of such a man?'

'No I bloody don't. But I wish I did.' Another pause. 'Are you saying there's doubts now – that it mayn't be Esau after all?'

Gently hung up, began to chew his sandwiches again.

Slatter said: 'Sir, you're not taking it seriously – what the chummie on the phone was giving us?'

Gently shook his head. 'Just following it up.'

But Slatter's eyes were more reproachful than ever.

'Cut along and see if he's finished his prayers.'

Slatter went. Gently finished his sandwiches. From the Chief Constable down to the reporters' night-watchman – everyone waiting for that climactic moment! And he, he alone uncertain, still haunted by the feeling of gaps unfilled: ready to snatch at a crank's phone call, reject Shaver's protégé outright. Why? The case was good enough, would certainly succeed. And yet . . .

Slatter returned.

'Is he off his knees?'

'Yes sir.' Slatter was beaming. 'Says God has spoken to him or some such cobblers, and now he's ready to face his accusers.'

'God has spoken . . .'

'Worth a quid in the box, sir. The Almighty has been telling him that he ought to confess.'

12

'And don't let the simple fisherman angle fool you . . .'

In his mind Capel's words were echoing when Lound was ushered through the door. All else aside: his appearance, religion, infatuation, eccentric style: they were dealing with a man of intelligence; wit lurked behind those staring eyes.

The warning was plain, yet one had to hold tight to it in the presence of that giant man.

'Sit, Lound.'

The same set-up as before, with the WPC busily sharpening her pencils, Slatter gazing at the prisoner with hungry eyes, the bruise on the constable's jaw a little darker. Only outside now the square was dark, the gapers all gone home.

'Lound, I am repeating my warning. What you say may be taken down and given in evidence.'

Even his posture had remained unchanged, the akimbo'd knees, still hands.

'Do you understand me?'

'I understand.'

'Is there anything you wish to say?'

'Before God I have prayed. He has given me enlightenment. It may be that in me has been abiding this evil.'

'Is that a confession?'

'Amen.'

'But are you guilty of the deaths of these two men?'

'In darkness I would have sworn the destruction of my soul. But now the darkness has been taken from me.'

'In so many words, Lound!'

'I do not know.'

'What?'

'I am dark in my understanding. But He has revealed to me that, now, I dare not swear to my total innocence.'

Well, that at least was an advance!

'Then to what will you swear?'

'To my ignorance of a perfect knowledge. Some things I remember, some I do not. I cannot swear upon the book.'

Gently stared. 'In other words, you are free to pitch us any sort of tale – it may be true, may be not, depending on how it's going down?'

Lound was unmoved.

'What I know I will tell.'

'Perhaps it would be better if you said nothing.'

'What is upon my soul must be said. Before, I spoke in ignorance of His will.'

'Then to get to cases! I'm asking you again, Lound – what were your movements on Sunday night?'

Just a flicker of the eyes.

'In darkness, few men will go to examine their nets. Of your ignorance of this I took advantage. The evil was upon me, and I lied.'

'You lied.'

He bowed his head.

'Then?'

'I am in this village. That I remember.'

'Doing what?'

'There were few lights. In just one house, a plain light there. A window at the side of a house. It may be that curtains were not pulled.'

'Your sister-in-law's house.'

'I am waiting.'

'You waited how long?'

He shook his head.

'Who did you see there?'

'I saw no man. I cannot say if one saw me.'

'You went to that window.'

Just the tiniest pause!

'It may be I did as you said. I cannot remember. If so, I was unobserved by those in the house.'

'You saw Barnby. Mrs Lound.'

'Nothing. Nothing I can remember.'

'Perhaps embracing, making love.'

'Nothing of that. Nothing.'

'Then, at last, he came out.'

'The darkness I remember, a great darkness. And the agony of my soul. And a relief, a great relief.'

'To put it no higher, you strangled Barnby.'

'A relief, as though I heard heavenly choirs.'

'Strangled him and left him hanging over the gate.'

'In my body a weakness, as though after much labour.'

Gently struck the desk. 'You killed that man!'

'All I remember I am telling.'

'And that won't do.'

For the first time, Lound's hands moved, making the big ring wink in the light.

'Don't let the simple fisherman angle fool you . . .'

Slatter, at least, wasn't being fooled. He sat staring at Lound with indignant eyes, clearly aching to get his word in. Lound was conning them! This wasn't a confession: just some bull which, later on, chummie would dodge out of – or, if it suited him better, make the basis of a manslaughter plea. After a moment, Slatter sat back, his eyes hooding, decided.

Gently said: 'You drove to Harford from Shinglebourne. Where do you say you parked your car?'

This time, a longer pause. At last:

'The place was close.'

'But where?'

Lound sat silent.

'Was it, for example, by the quay?'

Lound shook his head.

'On the square. The road to the house. At the Castle?'

'Close.'

'Then outside the house?'

'When I try to think, darkness.'

'You parked it, returned to it later, yet you have no knowledge of where you left it?'

'Perhaps, near the house.'

'Then not at the Castle?'

'I think, near the house.'

'Near the house,' Gently said. 'You parked. You walked along the road. You could see a lighted window in your sister-in-law's house. Tell me what else you could see.'

'This lighted window alone.'

'At no time was there a light in an upper window?'

The movement of a hand.

'I saw none.'

'Then a witness who saw such a light was mistaken?'

'I cannot answer for other men.'

'Tell me what you did next.'

'It may be that I entered the garden, since it is said.'

'By the small gate.'

He nodded.

'Was Barnby's car in the drive?'

The hand again.

'None of this I remember. But if it is said of me, that I accept.'

'You remembered entering by the gate.'

'Not that either. I am before the house, and nothing more. I waited, how long I cannot say, the night and my mind are both black.'

'So what was your purpose in going there, Lound?'

A shake of the head.

'But you had a purpose?'

'A feeling only. That evil is abroad. That there is a power which threatens Beatrice.'

'A power?'

'A power of evil.'

'Barnby?'

'A power perhaps not of man. And yet a power that was using him, using a man. Perhaps Barnby.'

'That is what you thought?'

'The power drew me. Outside the house I could feel it strongly. I knew I must stay, must wrestle with it, as Jacob wrestled with the angel.'

'So you wrestled. And won.'

'It was His will.'

'And Barnby was left hanging over the gate.'

'For that one bout the power was defeated. The outward sign may be as you say.'

'Once more, you strangled Barnby.'

'I remember the relief, and, as it seemed, the hosannas of the Throng.'

'Yet you took care to remove your ring before seizing him.'

His eye fell on it.

'I had the ring from my mother.'

Now Slatter was sitting forward again!

'You removed the ring.'

'It could be as you say.'

'Not because your mother gave it to you, but because it might leave an injury that could be identified.'

'My mind is dark.'

'But you removed the ring?'

'If it is alleged, I accept it.'

'I wish you to think very hard, Lound. Did you remove it?'

'It may be that I did.'

And he stirred the great hands with a trace of unease, though his staring eyes never faltered. Slatter was gazing now with an odd intentness, lips pressed tight; while even the WPC paused in her scribbling to throw Lound a curious little look.

Gently said:

'You drove home. No one witnessed your coming or going. Now we come to yesterday. Perhaps you will tell us what happened then.'

Lound said: 'I delivered fish.'

'Never mind about delivering fish!'

'In my soul, I felt the evil still threatening. I had scotched the snake, not killed it.'

'You rang your sister-in-law.'

'Beatrice was angered.'

'She told you to stay away from here.'

He sank his head.

'She feared for my safety. When she should have been fearing for her own.'

'Her own safety?'

'She stood in danger.'

'Danger from whom?'

'From the evil power. And I alone could be her shield and the protector of her soul.'

'You wished to offer her spiritual protection?'

The hands were in motion.

'Spiritual, bodily, it is the same.'

'But in whom was this threatening power embodied?'

'Perhaps, in many men.'

'Perhaps, in you.'

He drew a great sighing breath.

'Never in me. I have been her rock through every storm. Unto this one. And now again. When the evil she has provoked stalks abroad.'

'But, no longer.'

The hands. And a flicker in the eyes.

'Go on.'

'She was angered. Yet I came. Being in fear for her. I parked my car where it is said, wishing to approach unobserved. Another man was before me. Beatrice conversed with him at the door. The evil was in him, and she resisted it, sent this man on his way.'

'He returned to his car. Where was it parked?'

A pause!

'I do not recall.'

'A car parked by her gate. Wouldn't you have seen it?'

'I had not come to look for cars.'

'Yet if it were there?'

'In my memory, only the man who conversed at the door.'

'Go on.'

'It is as before, the darkness, the agony, the relief.'

'Only, this time, you forget to remove the ring.'

'It may be so, I cannot tell.'

'You wrestled with the angel.'

'With all my soul. And again I overcame. But next I remember only that I am sitting again in my car. I drove then, as is said, very fast, I do not recall the man turning his car, but this I accept. Also the youth said to have been there, and who picked me out.'

Gently said: 'Wait. You'll remember this. The man seen by the witnesses was wearing a cloak. Such a cloak I have seen at your house. Were you not wearing that cloak last night?'

'If it was seen –'

'I want you to remember.'

The eyes, the hands.

'It is God's will.'

'You were wearing it.'

The great head nodded.

'Then that's all for the moment.'

'All . . . ?'

'Take him out.'

'The lousy so-and-so – he didn't do it!'

'And you realise where that leaves us?'

In his excitement, Slatter had jumped to his feet, was gazing at Gently almost accusingly.

'All that Bible-thumping nonsense –!'

'Out there somewhere is another man.'

'I just can't believe it!'

'A man who is Lound's ringer – down to the signet ring on his finger.'

'A dead ringer . . . !'

Slatter's eyes opened wide.

'Exactly that. And there can be but one.'

'You can't mean –'

'Lound's brother.'

Slatter sat again with a bump.

'Can't be, sir!'

'Listen,' Gently said. 'The bearded yachtsman in The Mariners.'

'But someone would have recognised him –'

'Only they didn't. He's been thought dead for six years, probably altered in appearance.'

'But –'

'Call Bartram in.'

After a moment, Slatter jumped up again. Bartram came in looking flustered, eyes rounded with incredulity.

'Sir –!'

'Just listen. Didn't you see Aaron Lound set sail?'

'Yes sir, I did –'

'Then perhaps you can remember whether, in those days, he was clean-shaven?'

'Well yes, he was, sir. But –'

'So now he isn't. He's fully bearded. And six years later he appears in The Mariners and buys a pint from a landlord who has never met him.'

'But sir –'

'Listen. He's just another yachtsman, sitting alone with his pint. And round him the locals gossiping – what do you think they're gossiping about?'

'Oh crikey!' Slatter gaped.

'So he hears what he hears – carries on to the house, sees Barnby there making love to Mrs Lound – result, strangling one. The tide is wrong, he can't take off, has to wait for the morning ebb. But he was given out as dead six years ago, so what risk does he run, out there on the moorings?'

'But next he has a car, sir – a red car!'

'Follow him through. Shavers saw him make sail. He goes down-river on the ebb and catches the flood again, to Sheepbridge. There, he's on moorings all yesterday, and there he could very well rent a car. Maybe he came back to visit Mrs Lound, but what he happened on was Jackson. Strangling two.'

'And then . . . takes off again, sir?'

'On the morning ebb.'

'But he could be half-way to Holland by now, sir!'

Gently shook his head. 'The voice on the phone. He's out there now. His yacht's back on the moorings.'

'Out there now . . .'

'And stuck on a flood. But those calls were made in the village. One from the box on the quay, the other probably from the box right outside here. And Esau Lound, he knows, he's trying to cover for his brother, that's the only explanation. Esau is ready to take the rap.'

'All along, he knew his brother was back?'

'Knew. And was told to keep his mouth shut.'

'But in that case . . .'

The phone jangled. Gently snatched it up.

'Yes?'

'No need to snap at me!' Mrs Lound's slightly mellow voice. 'What I want to know is if that old lug is still being held at the police station.'

'Why do you ask?'

A hiccup. 'I'll tell you. That little wet Markie has been on the phone . . . something important to tell me, he says, just if he could talk round the door, like Jacko. Couldn't put the silly sod off.'

'When was this?'

'A minute ago. He'll be on his way now. Well, I thought I'd better check, make certain . . . don't want it all happening again, do we?'

'Thank you, Mrs Lound, we'll take care of it.' He hung up. 'Burrows is on his way to visit Mrs Lound.'

'Burrows!'

Bartram said: 'I'll send a car.'

Gently shook his head. 'No.'

'But if chummie catches him –!'

'It's chummie we want. A car covering the junction is all. Have you a man who knows the moorings?'

Bartram gulped, nodded.

'Send him with another man to cut chummie off there. Slatter, Cox, Abbot and myself will make an approach over the playing-field.'

'But if you're too late, sir –!'

'That's the risk, but we want that man. Let's go.'

'Spread out – and keep quiet.'

They had left unobserved by the reporters' night-watchman, now were entering the playing-field: so far, without meeting a soul. Ahead, a darkness almost complete, the sky scarcely discernible from the land: just the one small beacon-light shining from a window where curtains were unpulled.

Slatter whispered: 'If we run across Burrows, sir?'

'We hold back and let him rip.'

'Chummie could get to him first, sir.'

'Then we shout and run like bastards.'

But, as yet, no sign of anyone, no sound in the spacious dark; just the soft whisper of feet on grass as they moved swiftly towards the far gateway. Was Burrows coming? The odds were that he'd made his call from the box on the quay. In that case they should be ahead of him, must take care that he didn't spot them. Burrows was the bait . . . if he carried out his intention, could the tiger fail to pounce?

'Extra caution now.'

The black masses of the holm-oaks were fretting against the faint spread of light. Here, two nights running, Burrows had waited, caught glimpses of their quarry.

'Fade into this cover and wait.'

He, himself, crept out to the road. Visible the gates, the heavy shadow of the house, apron of turf and neglected flower-beds. And something to hear: Mrs Lound's gurgling laugh, a faint twitter of conversation. But nothing else. No sound of motion. The little scene was an island in the silence, in the night. Had he got it wrong?

Then Slatter was beside him:

'Quick, sir – someone coming!'

And only just in time he withdrew into the black lair of the holm-oaks. Footfalls; it had to be Burrows. They were holding their breaths as the feet went by. Then they could see the lanky figure moving against the web of light.

'Move up but keep cover.'

Four men edging towards the road. The wicket creaked – the sound was shattering! – and feet crunched on the gravel of the drive.

'Don't watch him – watch for chummie.'

Burrows was lost in the shadow of the house. Moments passed . . . what was he doing? . . . but, finally, the dulled sound of chimes.

'No sign of chummie, sir.'

'Keep watching!'

Only silence had followed the chimes. Silence in the house, silence outside. Then the chimes murmuring again.

'She's not going to play, sir . . .'

Several times the chimes, urgent. And at last the porch-light blazing overhead, to show the startled Burrows pulling back from the door.

'Watch – keep watching!'

Now the scene was better lit – drive, hedges, flower-beds, shrubs, the road. A lurking figure would have had to move swiftly to avoid that sudden spill of light. But as yet – nothing, sound, shape: if the fellow was there, where was he?

'She's not going to play . . .'

The door stayed shut. Burrows rang again and again. The chimes sounded mournfully, helplessly. Yet Mrs Lound was certainly in there.

Then, more light! The window above: she'd thrown up the sash, was glaring down at him.

'You sod. Can't you take no for an answer? Clear out, and stop ringing that pesky bell!'

'But . . . Beattie!'

'Never mind about Beattie – sling your hook this moment, do you hear?'

'Beattie . . .'

'Get lost.'

'But Beattie . . . I love you!'

'You what?'

'I want to marry you, Beattie!'

'To marry me!'

She threw back her head in a hoot of mocking laughter.

'Listen you soft sod, I eat little boys like you before breakfast. Don't think because I've given you a tumble that you can call yourself a grown man.'

'I . . . I love you!'

'You wouldn't know what it means.'

'I'll do anything for you, Beattie – I'll make up to you for all this.'

Another hoot.

'You and who else? You haven't grown out of your knee-pants, sonny. If I want a man I know where to get one, I don't have to snatch them from the cradle.'

'You don't mean that, Beattie.'

'Just sling your hook.'

'I'll be twenty next birthday –'

'Off home to mother, my little man, and stop playing games with my door-bell.'

'But I want to marry you –'

And then it happened. Around the white throat, something dark. Her mouth gaping, eyes popping, a great bearded head rising over hers. And the voice of another woman shrieking, shrieking, mingling with the curses of the man.

'The bugger's got in there!'

'Come on – through a window!'

Gently led the rush up the drive. In a flower-bed, a garden gnome: he sent it crashing through a pane of glass. They bundled through, made a dash for the stairs, at the top of which loomed a giant figure.

'Lound!'

The figure made to launch itself, feet first, at the men on the stairs: when a second figure leaped on its back, causing it to stagger and lose balance.

'Get him.'

Easier said than done, even though the Rivett woman still clawed on to him! Like trying to subdue a cornered gorilla, all threshing arms and kicking legs.

'. . . cuffs!'

It was Slatter who got them on, shackling first one great wrist, then the other. But would they hold him? At once he was clashing them together and jerking them apart in a ferocious manner.

'A rope . . . !'

Three of them sat on him while Abbot belted downstairs in search of one. The Rivett woman dodged back to the bedroom, then set up a wail:

'I think he's killed her!'

Abbot came back with a hank of clothes-line: Gently left them to pinion the man's arms. He hadn't killed Beattie Lound. She was sitting white-faced on the bed, feeling her throat.

'You know that man?'

'The bastard – the bastard!'

'But you know him?'

'Why couldn't he have drowned?'

'Is he Aaron Lound?'

'Bloody, bloody Aaron! Aaron bloody Lound. Bloody Aaron.'

And bloody he was, but with the blood of policemen who'd been cut when they blundered through the window. Now they'd got him to his feet, all ton of him, a panting, cursing, glaring giant, clad in a beige anorak, PVC trousers and yachting boots.

Bigger than his brother? It almost seemed so, with the bird's-nest beard framing the same features, the hooked nose, compressed mouth: only the hating eyes different.

And on a finger of the shackled hand, an identical ring, the present of a mother.

'Lound.'

He spat at Gently.

'I'm arresting you for double murder.'

The Rivett woman gave another wail. Then, in the doorway, Beattie Lound.

'You bugger. You were after me too.'

Lound spat at her. Missed.

She screamed: 'I'll tell you why they couldn't drown you – it's because somewhere, some day, you're going to be hanged!'

'Hush,' Gently said.

'He was going to kill me!'

Gently said: 'Did you mean to kill her, Lound?'

Lound spat sideways, leered at Beattie Lound, snarled:

'The bitch. She wasn't worth it, was she?'

More screaming!

'Get him downstairs.'

At the phone, he rang Bartram for transport. In the bedroom Beattie Lound was apparently having hysterics, with the Rivett woman trying to calm her down.

Then Burrows – they'd forgotten Burrows! Gently came upon him hovering by the wrecked window.

'Is she all right . . . ?'

Then he saw Lound, which was a pity.

'That's the man!'

Not that it mattered. Bartram had found them up a van, and also sent along WPC Joyce. While now they would have to turn out brother Esau, since the police station at Harford had only the one cell.

13

Still on his key-ring, after six years, the key that had let him into the house; about his waist a money-belt supplied with gold Kruger-rands; and on the moorings, crudely repainted, varnish blistered, but with new sails, the yacht which a band had played down-river, and which had not gone down in a typhoon season.

The chaplain of Norwich Prison it was who got the tale out of him. There had been typhoon trouble, oh yes! – twenty days out from Panama. Bare poles, huge seas, day black as night, no food or sleep for forty-eight hours: just hanging on, hanging on: the big Suffolk fisherman and the Pacific. And he'd ridden the storm, seen it off, collapsed dead with fatigue in the calm that followed, woke to find himself slummocking in a swell in a position he either never knew or wouldn't tell. Off an island! One of the Marquesas? The Tuamotu Archipelago? Just an island, a coral island. Somewhere in the Seven Seas.

And the canoes had come off to meet him, outriggers paddled by golden men, and they had gazed and jabbered as they circled the vessel that was bringing this huge man out of the sea.

'Kon-taku! Kon-taku!'

They had towed him in, brought him to a mooring in the lagoon, paddled him ashore and, capering and singing, led him to a village of palm-thatched huts.

'Kon-taku! Kon-taku!'

Came the women, the children, brought him garlands, fish, fruit: bowing, laughing, kneeling before him, while the men danced and sang. A hut with woven walls was his, a throne-chair carved with strange creatures: wifey-you's, take his pick! – and they were handsome maidens on that island.

'Kon-taku!'

After the hell of the sea, why not, why resist the workings of providence? Head and shoulders above the golden men, and now bearded like a Zeus, a Poseidon? They were fishermen, and such was he: their craft he understood, if not their language. Out there, deprivation, hardship: here, the feasting, the dancing, the wifey-you's!

And so he stayed on, their Kon-taku, their Fisher-King risen out of the sea, organising their fishing, their revels, and incidentally siring a few me-belonga-taku's. For five years, going on. When images long-suppressed began to assail him: of a woman left behind, of wealth once his, perhaps even of the taste of a Suffolk pint. Images suddenly a passion: he'd overhauled the yacht that still lay in the lagoon. And plunged the whole village into deep mourning as his sail stood away into the horizon.

He'd come to Port Darwin.

'Didn't you think to cable home?'

'Too busy refitting the boat, wasn't I?'

The same at Singapore and Penang, at Bombay, Suez and Tangier. Perhaps he'd guessed what was happening at home? At all events, no message. And finally his sail was going past Start Point, Beachy Head, and mingling with the cross-Channel ferries. Then, from Maldon, he'd rung his brother.

'Didn't you learn of the situation from him?'

'What, Esau? He's soft about Beattie. He just told me the bitch hadn't married again.'

And Esau he'd sworn to secrecy: Esau, who had never disobeyed his brother: and who was hoping, it may be, that if he kept his mouth shut, a reconciliation might be possible. Anyway, shut he'd kept it, and followed the fatal tide. At The Mariners some cockney wide-boy had served Aaron his pint, and no face had lit up in astonished recognition. And he'd heard what he'd heard. He'd gone back to the moorings, sat a while on the bank, watching the beacon; then he had gone up across the marshes and crept into the garden, up to the window.

'Had you no pity for that man, Aaron?'

'He was across her. On the settee.'

Kon-taku, the Fisher-King, had taken this old colleague by the throat.

Caution needed now! But his return from the dead was as yet known only to Esau. Safe to drop round to a mooring at Sheepbridge, rent a car, present himself again.

'Wouldn't it have been wiser to sail away?'

'That bitch was sitting on my house, my money. And who knows, we might have got together again. Once the business had blown over.'

'But after that second terrible crime?'

'I was going to see her, come what may.'

'Did you intend to harm her, Aaron?'

He'd shaken his head.

'Not then.'

Not then; not when entering the house; it was the passage with Burrows that had enraged him. And if in truth he had intended to kill his wife, would she not have been dead before any could have saved her?

'I shall pray for your soul, Aaron Lound.'

Kon-taku, the Fisher-King, bowed his head.

But that wasn't the end of the strange tale. His trial was scheduled for May, in the Norwich Crown Court. Gently had driven up for the first day from Heatherings, to be shown into an annex of the dreary Court One. As he sat patiently waiting for the court to assemble, he became aware of some commotion outside. A court messenger came rushing into the room, saw only Gently, and was about to rush out again. Gently grabbed him.

'What's going on?'

'An escaped prisoner! You haven't seen him . . . ?'

'Who?'

'The murderer, Lound. He knocked out the two officers sent to fetch him from the cells.'

And not only that. The cells at the Shirehall were connected to the courts by a narrow passage; it passed to the rear of a small courtyard where the judges and top officials parked their cars. Lound had smashed through a door as though it were paper and emerged into the courtyard, there to find a car, a BMW, with the key left in the ignition. Exit a Fisher-King. The car was found, some while later, in the park at the railway terminus. It had belonged to the judge who was about to try him. Missing from the glove compartment, cash.

'He won't get far!'

Well . . . only to Holland. At the weekend a yacht was missing at Pin Mill, to be reported in due course by the Dutch authorities as found illegally moored at Scheveningen. Gone away! A man you couldn't hide, but who somehow was managing to hide himself, perhaps among the riff-raff of Amsterdam, perhaps in Hamburg, or . . . just perhaps . . . ?

'A queer business, George. Dashed queer.'

That was Sir Tommy, KCB.

But Capel was able to give him the last word when, in June, he was lunching at Heatherings.

'Our Gentle Giant had acquired a housekeeper.'

'A housekeeper? Then he married his Beattie?'

'No – hadn't you heard? She sold her house, and now she's running The Eel's Foot along with Boy Markie.'

'Along with – whom?'

'Young Markie Burrows. They were hitched as soon as her divorce came through.'

Gently stared a long while.

'Then who is the housekeeper?'

'Guess, you old devil.'

And Mrs Burrows it was.

[Brundall, 1986/7]

NOTE

The above book was suggested to me by a Greek author, an old Seven Cities man, a bit of a rhymester.

A.H.